# A Girl, A Devil, and a Secret

## Christopher Lisenby

# Contents

# CHAPTER 1

A t night

Xin-ye was running on the street in school uniform while a young boy in the same school uniform was chasing her, after a while Xin-ye suddenly fell and got hurt. The boy who was chasing her was her twin younger brother... he was only 2 mins younger than her. Lin quickly came to Xin-ye and said can't you even walk/run properly, Xin-ye replied in an informal way -- I am older than you, you better give respect to me otherwise I will never help you... Lin: you are just 2min older than me.. Xin-ye - so what huh !Lin- nothing my sister come let's go home ( with a fake smile )Xin-ye said yeah let's goo my little bro.

Xin-ye was a little injured so she was walking slowly. while Lin was ahead of her... Xin-ye stepped on something and checked while saying what the hack is this.... and saw a beautiful necklace

.

Xin-ye: wowwww it's so pretty. Lin-whom are you talking to. can't you just walk a little faster. Xin-ye: bro look isn't it pretty. Lin- it is but where did you get this.It would be better if you didn't steal it from someone. Xin-ye : do you have a death wish ( about to beat him) I found it here under my feet. So, it's mine now ( happily wear it and showed to lin ) how is it looking on me. Lin - it looks like a trash is wearing a diamond. Xin-ye: whhhaattttt you bloody ( kicked lin ) and lin run. Xin-ye also ran to beat him, although Xin-ye was injured but she wanted to beat him so she didn't notice her wound.

They both reached home

Xin-ye and Lin reached home. Their mom was waiting for them so that she could ask them that...where they were at this late hour.Mom- both of you (stared) why are you late today ? Lin said mom Xin-ye fell on the road and was crying like a 2 year old kid (Xin-ye slapped on his head) xin-ye: mom he is lying I didn't cry. Mom - Xin-ye you fell on the road ( worried ) are you hurt ? Xin-ye - yes mom ( baby face ) my knees have been scratched, mom said Show me ..Xin-ye shows her knees but there were no sign of any wound/scratch. Mom - are you trying to fool me ( angry ) Xin ye - mom I swear that I fell on the road and I was hurt too. lin- mom sis is not lying this time I saw that her knee was scratched Mom- than where is the wound huh ! Xin-ye and Lin both were confused and was trying to figure out what is happening. Mom- I am leaving you today but it would be better if you guys stop fooling me by your lies. Xin-ye and Lin went to their rooms. Xin-ye was still thinking about it, how she fell and got hurt but now there is no sign of that Lin came to Xin-ye's room and asked, You were hurt right xin-ye replied hmm.

Lin: I am going to do something so please don't get angry on me pleaseeeee. Xin-ye: what are you going to do ( worried )Lin shows her the knife. Xin-ye said- what are you going to do with it,

I thought you were going to do something crazy but Lin- I am sorry my sis ( use the knife to make a small cut on her hand )Xin-ye: are you crazy or what huh and just ( kicked him ) Lin ( in painful voice because of her kick) hey look ( surprised and scared ) your hand is completely fine and the ( stammering ) b-blood where did it go and the c-cut. They both get scared.

# Chapter 2

Xin-ye: You wanted to kill me huh!.. Lin : xin-ye look at your hand Xin ( looked and got shocked ) and shouted ahhhhhhhh-hhhhhhh. Their mother came into the room and asked them: why are you making so much noise Lin covering Xin's mouth. And said- mom she just saw a lizard and got scared Xin-ye bites Lin's hand and says-- yes mom, he is right ( giving devil look to lin ) there was a lizard but now it's gone. Mom- If you both make more noise then, I will throw you out of the house. Okkkkk ( angry )

Mom leaves.

Xin-ye gives a deadly stare to lin. Lin got scared and said s-sorry I didn't do it to harm you Xin- what if i would have died. Lin( bothered )- stop overreacting it was just a little cut Xin -First you cut me with knife and now you are shouting at me. ( Lin in his mind : she is behaving like i have cut her into 1000 pieces ) Lin ( in a calm voice ) my dear sister, I am really very sorry it's all my fault ( fake smile ). ( Confused ) But how did you gain this kind to ability. They both started thinking.

Xin-ye and Lin started making different weird faces while thinking about how did she gain this kind of strange ability.

After 5-10 minutes

Suddenly Lin - I think I got it..( excitedly )Xin-ye :-what tell me ( curiously ). Lin smiled and said today you got hurt and then you got that necklace ( pointing at the necklace on xin's neck ). Xin-ye - do you really think that this necklace has this much capability huh! Xin-ye after thinking for a while : ummm Why don't we test it ( smirked ) Lin nervously asked what are you going to dooo. Xin-ye: I will do the same thing and smiles.

Lin - you did it on purpose right ( angry + annoyed ). Xin ( childish face ) didn't you just said that this necklace give me that weird ability. And start laughing.

A voice came from next door ( mom ) - do you wanna sleep on the road tonight........if not then sleep early....

NEXT DAY

Xin-ye and Lin leave for school early in the morning.

Lin- don't cause any kind of problem and don't ever tell anyone about your weird ability Xin-ye as an obedient child nodded hmm. They both leave for their classes Xin-ye seats with her bestie Yang Ximi, Xin wanted to share this secret with her but she controlled herself.

Class teacher ( miss Zeng ) comes in the class and everyone greets her - Good morning teacher Miss zeng - Good morning so, class Today we have a new tranfered students who will be your classmate from today onwards.

A boy enters from the entrance of the class...( Everyone started appreciating his looks )

Miss zeng - Introduce yourself to your new classmates.

BOY : My name is Lu Jing ( He isn't happy at all ) I hope you guys will not bother me ( Some girls : is he a rude person making annoyed faces but admiring his looks )

Miss zeng : Lu Jing, you can seat on the second last seat.

Lu Jing goes and sits on that seat.

Ximi : hey look he is so handsome Xin : ummmmmm he is handsome but very rude so, let's stay away from him Okie.

# CHAPTER 3

F ew days later

Xin-ye and Lin were going to school and a man came and showed them a knife and said whatever you have just give it to me ( In a scary voice ) Lin ( Attitude ) : we are students what do you think we have to give you. Xin ( in low voice ) : yaaaaa. Do you want us to die right now. Man: stop whispering and give me whatever you have. And also the thing that this girl is wearing ( Pointing at the necklace). Lin : We are not scared of you. Do whatever you can. ( He was scared to death but still was trying to be brave ) Xin-ye: Bro you are really my bro ( overacting ) yeah you thief or whatever he will fight with you ( Smile ) Lin gets more scared after hearing her words and looked at her ( in mind - I am sure you are not my sister. You want me to die. You have powers but you want me to fight with a man who has a knife.)

Suddenly a brick hit the head of the thief/man and the man fell on the ground.

Xin and Lin were shocked and looking at the brick. And then looked at the boy who was standing behind the thief/man. He was Lu Jing.After hitting the man he left. Xin-ye and Lin were just looking at him and were standing like a statue for a moment.

IN SCHOOL

Xin-ye wanted to say Thanks to him/Lu Jing but Lu Jing wasn't paying any attention to her. She knocked at his desk and said you didn't have to help us but still thank you so much ( Xin wanted to say it with some respect but it sounded a bit rude ). Lu Jing: If you want to thank me then come with me. Xin-ye: Whatt ( goes behind him ) where are we going? Xin-ye followed him.

Lu Jing and Xin-Ye come to the backyard. Lu Jing : you wanted to thank me right. ( Coming closer to her ) He was staring at the necklace on her neck and was about to snatch it...Xin-ye : can't you talk from a distance. ( giving wierd look ). Lu Jing: ummm I can't and tries to touch the necklace. The necklace flashed.

Lu Jing: So, you are the new owner.Xin-ye: what are you talking about. huh! And why did you touched my necklace ( In mind - why did the necklace flashed just now )

Lu Jing: I know you have some powers right now. Like -- you can't get hurt. You can move things with your powers. Xin: w-wait what do you mean. I can move things. ( Surprised+happy ). How can I move things ( curiously ). And how do you know all this things ( suspicious ).

Lu Jing: so you don't know much about your powers. And you don't know, what you are right now. Xin-ye: What do you mean by that? can't you just explain it in an easy way. (Pleasing face)Lu Jing: Why should I? Didn't you have your letter?? Xin-ye (confused): Huh! Letter. What letter. Lu Jing: Don't tell me that you didn't get your Letter. ( He started scarying her ). If you didn't get the letter- that means you are going to die very soon. Xin-ye : yaaa I am not a kid, you better not scare me. ( She was scared after hearing all this but was trying to be brave ) Lu Jing smiled mischievously after seeing her scared face.

Lu Jing : If don't want to die. Then find your letter so, that you can know everything about your powers.

Xin : wait.. You know so much about me and powers..( suspicious ). That means you also have this kind of powers right???Lu Jing didn't reply to her. But she was very curious to know about his powers. Lu Jing was about to leave. Xin-ye saw a piece of glass and tried to make a cut on Lu Jing's hand. And got shocked to see his blood. Xin-ye: y-you.. W-who are you??

# Chapter 4

Xin-ye made a cut on Lu Jing's hand. After that she saw his blood and got shocked. And asked w-who are you??

Xin-ye: you can't be a human being ( starting going backwards ). Lu Jing: I was a human. But right now ( deep voice ) I am a devil. But I want to become a human again. Xin-ye ( scared ): w-what are you s-saying. I literally don't understand anything. ( Xin wanted to run away but her body was numbed ).

Lu Jing: Do you remember the day when you found that necklace. Xin-ye ( nervously ) nodded...hmmmm....Lu Jing: The necklace is not normal. It is actually for the real guardian of his eyes moved and said- someone is here. Xin-ye: huh.....

In just a second they came outside their classroom.

Xin-ye( scared ) : W-we were in the b-backyard but now we are outside of our classroom how did we come here ( Looked right into his eyes ).

Lu Jing: Let's talk after the school. And walked away.

Xin-ye was just thinking about his black blood and what he just said to her there were so many questions in her mind.

AFTER THE SCHOOL

Xin-ye was waiting for Lin and wanted to run away from Lu Jing. But Lu Jing came and said : let's meet at 12 o'clock. Xin-ye: i won't come. Lu Jing: you don't have to Smirked and left.

Lin came and they both went to their house Lin has noticed that Xin-ye is worried about something. Lin: Is everything ok. If you are upset then. Tell me I will help you. You can even beat mee. Xin-ye: smiled for a bit but ( she was scared ) she trusts her brother more than anyone. She tells him everything about Lu Jing and what has happened today. Lin was a bit scared but didn't want to show it to xin-ye otherwise she will become more scared. Lin : So, he said that he will meet you at 12 o'clock. But he didn't said where. Xin-ye: hmmmm.

Xin-ye: one more thing he was talking about a letter but i don't know what kind of letter it is.

They both started finding letter. After one and half hours later they found 39 letters in their house. They started opening each and every letter.

After sometime they found a letter.

After reading this letter they both get scared+worried. Lin: Why do you had to pick this necklace. Xin-ye: w-wait that means (excited) now I am not a normal girl I will have powers and I will fight with demons woahhhhhhh it's gonna be so fun. Lin: ( worried) Are you out of your mind you will die. Xin-ye: I don't care I wanted some thrill in my life I was living a boring life but from now I will live an interesting life where I will fight and it will be so fun. Lin slaps on her head and said: I am going to tell everything to mom. Xin-ye: Yaaaaa please don't tell her anything. Lin was about to go but suddenly he became a statue he wasn't able to move.

Lin: xin-ye ( yelled ) what did you do to me. Xin-ye : wow is it my power. Isn't it cool. Lin: make me normal nowwwww. Xin-ye : firstly promise me that you will never tell mom or anyone about all this. Lin: ( bothered ) ok. But you also have to promise me. Whatever you do, you have to tell me everything. Xin-ye : ummm ok.

Lin become normal and now he can move. You can't use your powers on me. Xin-ye : Then whom will I test my powers on ( Smiled ).

It was about to be 12 o'clock.

Lin: It's about to be 12 o'clock. So, are you going to meet him or not. Xin-ye : He is a devil. What if he kills me. And I already have an excuse. That he didn't tell me where he is going to meet me. I am soo, smart ( being proud on herself ).

# CHAPTER 5

**1** 2 o'clock

Xin-ye: He is a deviL What if he killed me. And I already have an excuse. That he didn't tell me where he is going to meet me. I am so, smart ( being proud of herself ).

Lin : X-xin-yeeee ( low voice ) Xin : hmmm. Lin: L-lu Jing. He-he is behind you ( stummered ). Xin: huh ( Looked back ) and shocked to see lu Jing infornt of herself. Y-you. What are you doing here? ( clutching her necklace ). Lu Jing ( smirked ): oops… You got scared. Going closer to her. As you know that I want your necklace so, are you going to give it yourself or. Do you want me to take it by myself.

Lin was way to scared. And didn't know what to do. Then suddenly he says in a low voice : xin-yeee Xin-ye noticed him. Lin: Convert him into a statue, just like you did with me. Xin-ye understood what he tried to say. She used her powers on lu Jing. But that wasn't a success. Lin and Xin-ye. They both got nervous.

Lu Jing: I have more powers than you stupid. You don't even know, how to use the powers.( Smirking ). He tried to touch the necklace but the necklace flashed again and this time the necklace pushed him away. Lu Jing fell down from xin's room- window. Xin-ye's room is on the second floor. Xin-ye & lin - they go near to the window and nervously try to look down from the window. They were shocked after seeing that Lu Jing wasn't there.

Xin-ye : l-lin where did he go. Lin didn't reply. Xin-ye turned and saw that Lin isn't here. A sound comes (yearning voice) x-xin ye. H-help me.

Xin-ye looked outside from the window and saw that Lin is in the air and lu Jing is choking his neck. Lin was trying to say. Please help me. Xin-ye's eyes were filled with tears. And said I will give you this fu**ing necklace ( tears fall from her eyes ) leave my brother I promise I will give you.

Lu Jing: Do you really think that you can give me that necklace. Didn't you just read that this necklace is now connected with your life. Xin-ye : Then you just kill me and take this necklace. But please leave my brother. Lu Jing : I can't kill you. Because after killing you, I won't be able to become a human being again.

Xin-ye ( frustrated ): Then what do you want me to do ( crying ) I will help you. But please leave my brother ( Begging ).

Xin-ye wiping her tears I have an idea. Maybe you can become human again. But firstly you have to leave my brother and promise that you will never harm him. Lu Jing : how can I trust you.

I have that letter I can ask that letter for you.

Lu Jing safely left lin inside her room. Lu Jing: Now, ask that letter. How can I become a human.

Xin : ok

Xin-ye looked at him. Have you killed anyone?? Lu Jing: No Xin-ye: You know what I just helped you. If you had killed Lin. you wouldn't be able to become a human again. Lu Jing ( deadly starred ). Ask that letter. What's that way.

Xin-ye : why do I have to find demons for you. Lu Jing ( bothered ) : because you will have the wishes ( stupidddd ). How did you become a guardian.

Lin was unconscious.

Xin-ye : So, you can't kill anyone. Smiled. Now I don't have to be scared of you. Lu Jing; I can't kill anyone but i can hurt them. Do you want me to show you. Looked at lin.

Xin-ye: no no. Can we please start finding demons. From next month??? Lu Jing: No.... We will start from tomorrow. Xin-ye: ( high voice )WHAT. I don't even know how to use my powers. How can I face demons. What if they kill me to win this necklace.

# CHAPTER 6

Xin-ye : I don't even know what powers I have and how to use it. What if demons tries to kill me and win this necklace. Lu Jing : From now onwards I will protect you. So, don't even think of betraying me.

NEXT MORNING

Xin-ye didn't wanted to go to the school. So, she was behaving like she is sick. And Lin was supporting her in lies. Mom: ( worried) let me check what has happened to you. She uses a thermometer to check her temperature. Xin-ye's temperature was normal. That's why her mother got angry on her and asked her to go to school without making any trouble.

Xin-ye and Lin are on their way to school.

Lin : ( worried ) what will you do now. Xin-ye : ( nervously ) I can't even afford to ignore him. He is more powerful than me. I don't even know how to use my powers.. ahhhhhhhhhhhh.. Why do I have to help himmmmmmmm. Lin : I don't have any powers but. I will help you. I will try my best to protect you. ( Smiles nervously

). Xin-ye : Firstly protect yourself. Any try to stay away from that devil.

In School

Lin and Xin-ye go to their classrooms. Xin-ye waves her hand ( hey ) to Lu Jing who was staring at her. But he didn't react. Xi-ye goes and sits with Ximi ( bestfriend & deskmate ).

Class Teacher comes

Everyone stands and greets her. After a while. Teacher : Students today I am going to change your seats. Everyone : ahhhhh noooooo Mis Zeng. Please. Mis Zeng ( teacher ) - Our class performance is getting more and more worst than before. Today I will change your seats. But if you want to seat with your friends than get better marks in upcoming exam.

Miss Zeng arranged everyones seats.

Xin-ye's new deskmate is Lu Jing. Xin-ye : did you do all these things. Lu Jing : It's better to seat here. Xin-ye : huhhh! Your powers are really amazing. I wish I could use mine. Lu Jing : You will use it today ( smirked ). I have found a demon ( whispered ). He is in this class. Xin-ye ( shocked ) and shouted - whatttttttt. Mis Zeng : xin-yeeee do wanna stand outside in the first period. If not then sit quietly and answer these questions I will check your answers first. You have 20 mins. Xin-ye : O-Ok miss. Xin-ye looked at Lu Jing and gave him an angry look.

Xin-ye started solving questions. She didn't asked for any help to Lu Jing or others. She did it in just 15-17 mins. Xin-ye stands and says: Miss Zeng... I have done Miss Zeng checks her answers. Umm good Miss Zeng checks other students answere.

Xin-ye looked at Lu Jing ( in mind - You devil.... I will surely kill you one day ) fake smile : Are you sure that. You have found a demon and it's in this classroom. Lu Jing ( devil smile ) : just wait for the Sports period. Today you are not taking that period. Xin-ye: ( angry ) That's my favorite period. ( Childish ) Can we do all these demons and whatever after that period. Please. Lu Jing : smiling. No.

Xin-ye ( in mind ) why do I have to do things according to him. Wanted to beat him.

After some time everyone was going to the ground for sports period. Ximi : xin-ye let's go. Xin-ye: I am not going today I have headache. Ximi: you never skip this period. Are you ok. I will stay with you. Xin-ye ( panicked ) : N-no no. You go. Otherwise I will feel guilty for you. Please go. Ximi didn't want to go but xin-ye forced her to go. Everyone left the class.

Now, Only Lu Jing and xin-ye are in the classroom.

Xin-ye: there is no-one except us. Where is that so called demon. Lu Jing : it's behind you. Xin-ye got scared and didn't want to turn back. But slowly slowly turns and sees that there is only a flower vase. Xin-ye: ( angry+ high voice ) Why am I not able to see that fu**in* demon. If you are trying to scare me then stop here I have already skipped my fav period for you. So, it's better you don't bother me. Lu Jing: Do you really think that I have time for all this. A sound comes : Heyy Miss new Guardian. Nice to meet you.

# CHAPTER 7

A voice comes from the back of Xin-ye: Hey miss NEW GUARDIAN.

Xin-ye turned back. No one was there. She looked at Lu Jing. Why are you trying to scare me I am doing all this for you. Lu Jing : It's not me. Voice : It's me I am Mr. Flower. Xin-ye : ( surprised ) huh!.. Who.. Mr. flower.. She laughed. Yaaa lu Jing. Don't you have some better names. What kind of name is this Mr. Flower ( Laughing ). Suddenly she feels like something is touching her legs. She looked at her legs and got scared and screamed.. Ahhhhhhhhhhhh ( nervously ) what is this?

Mr. Flower : See it's me Mr. Flower. Xin-ye : Are you a demon ( In mind : I thought demons are scary ) Lu Jing : Didn't I tell you. There is a demon. Xin-ye : But how. How can this flower be a demon. It was grown two months ago. How can this become a demon. It must be you. You have powers you can do anything right. You are trying to fooling me.

Lu Jing : ( grinding teeth ) Why is this stupid is a guardian. Have you ever seen a demon before?

Xin-ye: hmmm so many times.. I have seen so many demons in movies , dramas , series, cartoon.. Mr. Flower ( angry ) : Can you stop it. It's me. And i am a demon. Do you want me to prove that to you. Xin-ye ( without thinking anything / casually ) - ummmmm I think you should prove yourself and ( being happy after saying all this ).

Mr. Flower : look I will give water my self with my powers. Xin-ye : umm w-wait I think giving water to yourself won't be that hard. So, I think ( acting like she is thinking ) you should give water to all the other plants of this school Mr. Flower : ok fine. Look outside the window. [ The weather changed and it started raining ] Xin-ye : It's not you. It's weather. I don't believe that you did this. Annoyed face. [ Rain stopped ]Xin-ye : I think you should do something like.. ( Thinking ) ummmm.. I got it.. You should treat that plant ( point outside of the window at a plant which wasn't growing well ). She smiled with satisfaction.

Mr. Flower treats that plant and says : look. Now it's growing. Xin-ye looks at the plant and smiles. I think you are a demon. But..

Lu Jing & Mr. Flower at a same time : what but. Lu Jing : what do you want now.

Xin-ye : goes closer to lu Jing whispered : Just wait for some more minutes. And stop the other classmates from coming inside this classroom. They must be coming to the class. It rained a few minutes ago.

Lu Jing : They are not coming here. And what proof do you want from that flower. Xin-ye : keep your voice a little low. Don't you remember we need to make the demon do 3 good deeds ( Smiles ). Yeah I know I am so smart. Lu Jing's expression changes. Oh ok done it faster. Xin-ye can't you even appreciate me. What a weirdo.

Mr. Flower : what are you two whispering.. ( Suspicious voice ) Xin-ye : we are trying to find a Difficult task for you Mr. Flower : I have an idea I will kill and take this necklace from you. Aren't this is the difficult task right now ( Laugh ). Xin-ye got a bit scared and looked at Lu Jing. Lu Jing was already looking at her.

Lu Jing : ( serious face ) Do you know who I am ? Mr. Flower : You. You are her boyfriend. No. You are not scared of me. You can't be a human. Are you. A demon tooo. Laugh. Lu Jing : neither her boyfriend nor demon. I am ( shows his hand - fire flames ).

Mr. Flower ( scared ) : Are you. Devil. No. But.. Why are you helping her. Lu Jing : it's none of your business. Just do as she says. Otherwise I will burn you.

Mr. Flower: You are a kiddo. You can't do this ( Lu Jing goes closer to that flower and was about to touch him ). Stoppppp. I will do. Whatever she will ask me to do. ( Disappointed voice ) Tell me what I have to do. Xin-ye : What should I ask him to do. Thinking seriously.

# Chapter 8

Xin-ye : what should I ask him to do. Thinking seriously. After a while she asked Mr. Flower to spread his fragrance so that everyone's mind can relax for a while Mr.Flower wasn't willing to do it. But Lu Jing was staring him Mr. Flower does as xin-ye said.

Everyone in the school smells that fragrance and feels refreshing. Those who were tired. They started doing their work.

Xin-ye's necklace shines for a moment. Xin-ye smiled. And looked at Lu Jing with satisfaction.

Lu Jing : Mr Flower. You have to go from here. And he just snapped his finger and that flower vase disappeared. Xin-ye was surprised and Claps for him. Xin-ye : Although I am the guardian of this necklace but I don't have powers yet. And look at you. You are a devil and still your powers are so amazing. I wish my powers to be more stronger and amazing than you. By the way where did he go. Lu Jing: He's gone where he should be. Smirked. Now we have to find more demons we have only found one. Xin-ye ; hmmmm now, we have to find only 998 demons more. It will be so fun.

Lu Jing : ( in mind ) Only 998. How can she think that it's just only 998. She isn't reliable. ( Annoyed ).

After sometime

Everyone comes to the class room. Ximi : xin-ye Are you ok ( worried )[ Xin-ye's head was down on the desk. ]Xin-ye : I am ok.. Don't worry  ( I wish I could tell you everything. A bit sad ).

After school. Xin-ye came home with her brother and tells him everything. Lin was worried because Lu Jing's power's are way too dangerous. Lin : Listen don't be dependent on him and try to avoid him as much as you can. He can be too dangerous. And those things ( weird ) Demons don't make fun of them like you did today. What if that thing tries to kill you. ( Xin-ye was listening to him but wasn't paying any attention. She was just thinking about his powers which were too cool for her ).

Xin-ye : Lin.. Leave it.. Let's test my power. Lin : Have you even heard what I just said now. Xin-ye: I have heard everything. ( Smiled ) now please. Let's test my powers. I wanna see if I have any new powers.

Xin-ye - snapped her fingers but nothing happened. She tried to make him a statue as she did before with him she was successful in making him a statue. But she didn't find any new powers in herself.

After some time she had her dinner.

At night she wasn't able to sleep. She was just disappointed because she don't have any other power. She was just thinking about all this. It was already 2am. Xin-ye heard a sound - MEOW, MEOW. She gets up and see that. There is a very cute cat outside her house. She started watching that cat. The cat was also doing cute things that makes xin-ye smiled. Xin-ye wanted to play with that cat. So, she quietly goes outside of the house.

She tries to touch the cat. Cat willingly comes closer to her and now down his head towards Xin-ye's hand. Xin-ye was happy to see that the cat is very comfortable with her. She took that cat with herself and went to her room silently/quietly.

She just played with that cat all night. She even give a name to that cat. [ It's a male cat ] HARRY. Xin-ye named him Harry.

Next Morning

Xin-ye didn't tell about Harry to Lin.

After few days. Nobody knows that xin-ye is petting a cat. She gives Harry food secretly.

One dayXin-ye went to school. Lu Jing : I don't know why but I can feel that a demon is very near to me. And looks at xin-ye. This feeling started when you entered the classroom. Xin-ye ( a bit rude ) : What do you mean by this. I always come to school. Then how can you say that.

Teacher comes and asks everyone to open their books.

Xin-ye opens her bag chain and got surprised.

# CHAPTER 9

Xin-ye opens her bag chain. She was surprised to see. That Harry was inside the bag and was looking at her with his adorable eyes. Xin-ye panicked and closed the chain ( She left the chain a bit open so that Harry can breath ). Lu Jing looks at her. Xin-ye gives a fake smile.

Teacher asked xin-ye where is your English book. Xin-ye ( nervously ) : um... Miss I forgot to bring my book. Teacher taunt her saying. Your grades are not that good in any subject except Maths. Being good in maths will not make you pass in every subject. And after 2 years you will be in college.

Xin-ye doesn't care what teacher said. She was just thinking of hiding Harry from everyone.

In Lunch break.

Ximi : Xin-ye. Let's go to the canteen. Xin-ye : ok.. Let's go.. ( In mind : I hope you don't make a sound Harry I will surely bring something for you to eat).

Lu Jing's gut feelings were getting more and more accurate ( Classroom was empty ) Lu Jing started scaning whole classroom with his powers. After a while He noticed that something is inside Xin-ye's bag. He opened it. He becomes suspicious after seeing her English book. ( Harry wasn't inside her bag).

After Lunch.

Xin-ye and other students come to the classroom. Lu Jing was staring at xin-ye. Xin-ye was confused. Lu Jing : Why did you lie today. Xin-ye ( frankly ) : About what?? Lu Jing throws her English book on the desk. About this. Xin-ye ( a bit angry ) : Why did you open my bag. Don't you have manners. Xin-ye opens her to check if Harry is okay or not. When she opened her Harry wasn't there. Xin-ye : where is that cat. Lu Jing : CAT.. What cat ( Looks away ). Xin-ye ( trying to hold her anger ) : I am asking you. Where is my cat Harry. Lu Jing didn't reply. Xin-ye left the classroom in anger. And started finding Harry.

The Next subject teacher comes to the class and started teaching. Lu Jing noticed that xin-ye is not in the classroom. And his senses were saying that a demon is near her. He also left the classroom. And started finding xin-ye.

Lu Jing heard some sound and followed them. After sometime he sees that Xin-ye was kneeling down and talking to someone. Lu Jing goes near to her and saw a cat. Xin-ye was petting that cat. Xin-ye saw lu Jing. What are you doing here ( angry ).Lu Jing : Stay away from that cat. It's not a cat. Harry tries attacks on Lu Jing. Xin-ye ( politely ) : Harry be a good boy. He is my friend.. Harry : A FRIEND. Xin-ye got shocked after hearing this ( Stammered ) You can talk. Lu Jing : Used his powers but Harry didn't got hurt. Harry : Xin-ye you are the best. I will never harm you. Lu Jing : You are a demon not a cat. Harry goes closer to xin-ye. Harry : I know what you need. I will surely do 3 good deeds. And i will also help you to find more demons. Please don't leave. I want to be with you ( emotionally ). Lu Jing was about to attack Harry. But suddenly a white light stopped him. ( Xin-ye made a protection layer around herself and Harry ).

Lu Jing & xin-ye both were stunned for a moment. Xin-ye : is it me. Who did this. Harry : Thank you xin-ye. You have protected me. From this devil. I will always be there for you. Lu Jing : How can we believe you. You are a demon. And I am 100% sure that you are here for this necklace.

Harry : I don't want that necklace. I just want to be with xin-ye. If you don't believe me then I can prove you. There is a place called --lie/truth detector--- we can go there. It's near Xin-ye's house. I can prove there that I am not lying.

Lu Jing : How can I believe you that it's not a trap. Harry gives his neck belt to lu Jing ( Giving neck belt is a sign that this pet can't harm you no matter what. If the pet tries to harm you he will disappear in a sec ). Xin-ye : We will go there. Looks at Harry - I don't want to loose you my friend. Harry becomes happy after hearing that she doesn't want to loose him. He started dancing in a cat way.

After school.

Xin-ye, Lu Jing, Lin and Harry went to that place. Lu Jing : Why did you bring this human here? Xin-ye : He wanted to come with me. And my mom won't allow me to go anywhere that easily.

Harry : It's the place ( It's a very silent place. Whole place is surrounded by trees ). Harry : Meowwwwww meowwwww we are here to test Lie/Truth please help us. In a while. A pond started coming out from the ground. The ground started shaking.

# Chapter 10

Harry : Meowwwww meowwwww we are here to test Lie/Truth please help us. In a while. A pond started coming out from the ground. The ground started shaking.

The pond was filled with transparent liquid. Harry : If I lie then the color of this liquid will turn into Black And if I am saying the truth then the color will be White. Lu Jing : Go ahead.

Harry : Meow Meow.... I am Harry and I want to test my loyalty. Pond ( very calm voice ) : Hello Meow Harry. You have to come forward and take a sip of my pond's liquid. And say something. Then this liquid will change its colour as black - Lie and white - Truth.. Harry takes a sip of the liquid : I am loyal towards Xin-ye.. And i will never harm her I want to be with her as a friend.

Pond's liquid colour started changing. Everyone's eyes are stuck on the liquid's colour. Colour changes and it's white. Xin-ye with a happy face : Harry you didn't lie. Harry goes closer to xin-ye. : Xin-ye.... Can I stay with you.

Lin ( surprised ) : What ?? You will live with us. Xin-ye ( deadly stared ) : Yes. And you can't tell anyone about him.

Harry ( a cold ) : What about you devil. Do you believe me or not? Lu Jing : Do you really think that I will believe a demon. And this pond.

Pond : How dare you to not believe on my liquid. Pond becomes angry. And all trees stems started moving across them. A tree grabs Lin's leg and pulls him upward ( hanging in air ). Xin-ye didn't know what to do : Lin try to get off your feet. Harry : Lu Jing. Devil. Give me my belt. Without that belt I can't help you. quickly give it to me.

Lu Jing was struggling because trees have covered him inside their stem. But he managed to give him his belt. Harry : xin-ye run. I will save them. Xin-ye : No matter what but i can't leave you guys. And look these trees are not coming closer to mee. They are just trying to harm you three ( suspiciously ). But why isn't it coming closer to me. Lu Jing ( his mouth was covered with stems ) : n-e-c-k-l-a-c-e. Xin-ye : I can't hear you. Are you saying necklace. She looks at her necklace. Harry started cutting stems with his teeth. But it wasn't working that well because there are so many trees and they all are trying to hurt them.

Xin-ye touchs her necklace. ( Worried ) : I don't even know it works but I still hope that it can stop right here. The letter appears right in front of her. She was surprised to see the letter. Lin : xin-ye ask that letter how can we get rid of these ( Painful voice ) Faster.

[ Lu Jing has been dragged inside the ground by the trees]

Xin-ye ( bothered ) : we have to find a key.. Ahhhhh. Now, where do I find this key in such a big forest. Harry : We will find it. But you have to make that layer around me & lin. This time I will try to bring Lin down then you make that layer. So, that I can scan this area. Xin-ye : But I don't know how to make that layer. But I will try my best. Harry uses his powers and Lin comes down to the ground. Harry : NOW. Make that protection layer. Xin-ye was struggling but in end she made the layer on time. Harry started scanning whole area and said: I think it's inside around that tree ( Pointing at a tree ) Xin-ye : I will go there. You guys stay here. Lin : What if they try to harm you. Xin-ye : They won't. And even if they try to harm. My wounds will disappear.

Xin-ye goes near that tree. Other trees weren't harming her. She saw a key around the tree. Xin-ye touchs the key. And suddenly every trees stem started coming closer to her. And a tree was about to fall on her ( xin-ye closed her eyes ). But Lu Jing grabbed her hand and pulled her. ( Xin-ye opens her eyes and looks at lu Jing ). Lu Jing : RUN. Towards the protection layer. Rum faster ( Stems were chasing them ). They both come inside the protective layer. Lin & Harry : Are you ok. ( Check her if she is fine ). And how did you come out from there. Lu Jing : I am way too stronger than these trees. Xin-ye : Then why did you run just now. Why don't you destroy them. ( Xin-ye noticed that lu Jing's hand is bleeding and the blood colour is black ). Xin-ye : Jokes are apart. Are you ok. Checks his hand.

Their layer started breaking. All the trees were attacking on the layer.

Lin : Arghhhhh I think we are going to die today. Lu Jing wanted to use his powers but xin-ye stops him saying. : You are injured and there are more than 1000 trees. Leave them on me.

Everyone ( together ) : Leave them on youuuuu. Xin-ye : Yup ( Smiles ) And shows them key I have got it. Xin-ye gives the key to lu jing and ask him to apologise to the pond. Lu Jing : I won't. Xin-ye : If you want to die then die alone. But we have to go back to our house. Otherwise my mom will surely kill us today. So, quickly throw it inside the pond and apologize. Okkkk.

# CHAPTER 11

Xin-ye : Ahhhhhh you Devil. Do it faster otherwise.

Lu Jing throws that key. ( A bit rudely ) : Sorry I shouldn't have said those words. The forest suddenly calms down and the trees stop attacking them.

Pond : It's better if you behave yourself. Pond disappeared.

Xin-ye checks Lu Jing if his hand is still bleeding. And found that his wounds have disappeared : It's good that you have healed yourself. Lin : He is Devil his wounds would have healed faster ( in pain ) But what about me I can feel the pain my legs ache I will never go with you guys anywhere ( pointing his finger on them and tried to walk but fell on the ground ). Xin-ye : laughs on him. Awwwww my little brother. Does it hurt that much. Lin : Don't you dare to make fun of me. Otherwise. I will tell mom about this cat.

Harry ( looks at Lin with anger ) : I was the one who helped you when you were swinging in the sky. And now you are betraying me I think. Lin : No no don't think anything I won't tell anyone about you ( Childish face + begging ) Let's go home. It's getting dark ( In mind : where did i get stuck. Ahhhh one is the devil ( looks at lu

Jing ) one is a demon cat ( looks at Harry )  and one the weirdest person, who is my sister but I don't think she is my sister ( passed a bitter smile to xin-ye ).

THEY REACH THEIR HOME.

Xin-ye & Lin tries to enter inside the house secretly. But their mom was waiting for them. Xin-ye quickly hides Harry behind her. Mom ( angry ): You both don't you think that you have come home very early.

Xin-ye : Mom. Actually. Mom : You just shut up ( shouted ). I got a call from your teacher today. She told me that you didn't bring your books and. You even bunked the classes today. Other teachers were also complaining that your grades are not that good.

Lin looks at xin-ye and whispered : No one can save you right now. ( Nodded in no ). Xin ( bothered ) : Mommmmm I wil do hard work. Mom : Hardwork and you. ( Bitterly smirked ) ( she wanted to slap her but). Lin : ( yelled ) Mom. My legs. He fell on the floor. Xin-ye & her mom hurriedly goes closer to Lin. Mom : What happened to you. ( She unfold his jeans.......)  And asked Xin-ye : where did you both go. tell me the truth. And how did he got hurt so badly.

Xin-ye was about to tell her everything because Lin's condition wasn't looking good. Xin-ye : mom actually we went to. Lin cutting her words. Lin : Mom actually. Today when we went out to play. We saw a cat that was about to get into a car accident. So, we saved him and I got hurt ( Lin winked at Xin-ye  ).

Mom : Are you sure you guys are not lying. Xin-ye ( nervously and a bit scared ) : mom we have brought that cat you can see Xin-ye moves aside Harry: meowwwww meow. Mom : why did you brought that cat here ( She is scared of cats ).

Suddenly door opens. Everyone looks at the door. A man entered and got a bit shocked : what are you guys doing here. Lin and xin-ye : Daddd.. Finally you come back from your business trip. Dad : Yeah I am back my child. And saw the cat ( Blinking his eyes rapidly ) Is it a cat.

At dining Table. Dad : so you guys want this cat to stay here. At our house. ( Whispered ) don't you guys know that your mom is scared of cats. Mom : who is scared of cat I am not scared of cat ( looks at cat who was sitting beside xin-ye). After some conversation mom and dad let Harry stay with them.

NEXT MORNING

Xin-ye was sleeping peacefully. But suddenly her door knocked Xin-ye didn't respond. Mom ( yelled ) : xin-ye get up. Xin-ye : mom it's Sunday. Let me sleep more. Mom : If you don't want me to throw that cat away then get up and come down. I have some plans for you.

xin-ye gets up and arghhhhhhhhh Xin-ye took a bath and goes down.

Mom : I have arranged a tutor for you Xin-ye : Mommmmm. But I. Mom : Your grades are going down day by day the tutor will come here in an hour. Be ready for it. Xin-ye : ok fine.  But mom where is Lin?? I haven't seen him today. Mom : He went to the doctor with dad. His legs were swelling. Xin-ye : ohh ( in mind :  He must be in pain. What a poor guy).

After an hour. The door bell rings.  Xin-ye opens the door. A beautiful lady was standing there. Xin-ye ( politely ) : My mom isn't at home. Lady : Are you xin-ye I am your new tutor. My name is MEI LIEN ( Smiles ) Xin-ye (in mind : oh shit how did i forget that Ahhhhh mom ).  Xin-ye : Please come in. Mei Lien was talking to her very politely. Xin-ye got comfortable with her. Mei Lien : You are really very good in maths. And for other subjects I will help you. Don't be pressurized.

# CHAPTER 12

**M**ei Lien makes her feel comfortable. So, that she can ask her doubts.

After 2 Hours.

Mei Lien : Xin-ye you are not bad in studies you just need to understand things and relate it to the reality. Xin-ye was happy to hear these words because no-one has ever appreciated her.

Mei Lien : Now, I have to go. I will come again tomorrow. If you have any queries then you can also call me. It's my number 98******70. Xin-ye : Ok Miss ( Smiles ) Bye.

After a few minutes.

Lu Jing comes to her house. Xin-ye thought that her parents had come back with Lin from the hospital. She opens the door.

Xin-ye : What are you doing here?? ( With a weird look ). Lu Jing : Don't forget that we have to find demons ( hold her hand ) Come with me Xin-ye tries to release her hands saying : Ahhhh leave my hand. Right now nobody is at home. What if my parents come home and don't find me at home?

Lu Jing : ( His eyes were a bit scary ) Either you come with me or I may bring the demons here. Xin-ye : Ok I will. Harry can you stay at home and inform me whether my parents are home or not? Harry : But I wanted to go with you ( a bit sad ).

Lu Jing & Xin-ye both leave the house.

After sometime they reach to a park.

Xin-ye : what are we doing here ?? Didn't you say that we have to find demons. Lu Jing : ( smirked )Do you know how many demons there are? Xin-ye ( a bit nervous ) : Demons and here ( Take it as a joke ) Not possible. Suddenly her expression changes. Are you serious?? She tries to go back but Lu Jing holds her hand. Lu Jing : You can't go back. Come with me.

Xin-ye ( whispers ) : Hey. How many demons are here exactly? Lu Jing : Around 156. Xin-ye ( stops for a moment and was way too shocked ) : 156. Wahttttt so many demons. I will never come here. No never. Lu Jing : Stop your nonsense. And follow me.

Lu Jing : Sit on this bench. Xin-ye was confused but she sits there. Lu Jing sits next to her.

The bench started spinning. After a moment it stopped. Xin-ye : Ahhhhhhhhh my headddd. It's like a mini heart attack.

Lu Jing grabs Xin-ye's hand and says : Don't leave my hands. Otherwise you will surely die. Xin-ye ( annoyed ) : ( talking to herself ) What have I done even after being alive now, my life is always in danger. Wait... what place is this. Looks around ( Got scared ). Why does it look like a creepy place. Lu Jing : Be ready. There are more than 150 demons and don't leave my hands. Now I will bring everyone here one by one in front of you ( Looks at her ) don't get scared.

Xin-ye was being more and more confused. Xin-ye ( in mind : I am dreaming or what. Whatever just see what's happening after all he won't let me die) : Ok Mr Devil ( in mind : I hope this whole game will end soon).

Lu Jing : Every one come one by one. Xin-ye got shocked : Are you crazy you are asking them to come. And do you really think that they will obey you. Lu Jing gives a devil Stare: Have you forgotten that I am Devil. More stronger than these demons.

Every time when someone comes in front of xin-ye. Her necklace flashes.

Xin-ye : something is strange. They have to do 3 good things but they aren't even doing anything. Then how. Lu Jing : They have done more than 3 good things. Xin-ye : Huh!! When did they do more than 3 good things. Lu Jing : These demons are not bad. They all are kind and have a helping nature. That's why they aren't attacking you. Xin-ye : ohhhhhhhhhhhhh ( her fear vanished and a smile appears on her face k.. ( In mind : So, not all demons are bad. This world is really something. If there are bad people, then there are good people too ).

After sometime.

Lu Jing : All of you thank you so much. Xin-ye ( in mind : Did he thanked them. Woahh I didn't expect that he could have thanked anyone ) : All of thank you so much. Have a good life.

Xin-ye : Can we go now?? Lu Jing : Be ready to have a mini heart attack. Xin-ye : againnn.. Ahhh.. Ok.. I am ready.

The bench spins.

Xin-ye reached her house. Opens the door silently. Harry ( happily ) : xin-ye you are back. Xin-ye ( whispers ) : Are my parents at home?? Harry : ( nodded in no ). Xin-ye : They haven't come back yet. She called her mom. Mom : Hello, xin-ye. Xin-ye : Mom where are you? And why didn't you come back yet? Mom : xin-ye I don't think we'll be able to come home today. You have to stay at home alone for tonight. Xin-ye ( serious ) : Mom. Is Lin ok. Mom : He is okay. But his leg is fractured. Dr. Have advised him to stay here for tonight maybe your dad will come to you at night. Don't worry about us. Just stay safe ok. Xin-ye : Ohh..... Ok mom. Take care of Lin and yourself.

Xin-ye started overthinking. Lin is injured because of me I shouldn't have taken him with me ( Her eyes started filling with tears).

Harry : It's not your fault Xin-ye. You are not a bad person.

At night her dad came back. Xin-ye went to sleep in her room.

In her dreams. She saw a creepy woman who was holding someone's head and her hands were full of blood. That creepy woman was running towards Xin-ye. Xin-ye screamed.

# CHAPTER 13

Xin-ye screamed she was very scared her face was completely red.

Dad & Harry They both wake up and go to Xin-ye. Dad hugs her and says : What happened. Are you alright. Harry : Meowwwwww meowwwww.

Xin-ye was way too scared she was trying to say but couldn't. She started crying. Dad was worried for her: xin-ye. My child you must have had a bad dream. Don't be scared I am with you ( Xin-ye she was trembling all over ).

no one sleeps tonight.

Next Morning

Xin-ye was holding her dad and her dad was taking a nap. Xin-ye feels that someone had opened the door of her house. Xin-ye wakes up her dad : Dad someone had opened the main door. Dad please go and check.

Dad goes and sees he saw that it was his wife and his son.

After sometime

Xin-ye came down. Mom ( politely ) : what happened to you last night Lin ( teased ) : mom she must be faking. Xin-ye hugs her mother. Her eyes were swollen Lin ( a lit low voice ) : ohh so you weren't faking. Her Mom got more worried because xin-ye usually don't hug anyone.

It's been 3 days.

Xin-ye had the same dream every night and she could not even sleep at night.

Everyone was worried for her she wasn't even going to school but her tutor used to come daily to teach her.

Harry ( When nobody was near him & xin-ye ) : xin-ye I wanted to do it earlier but I couldn t because you weren't alone. Xin-ye : What do you mean?? What you wanted to do Harry : can you tell me about that dream. Actually cats eyes can see anything. And I am a demon so my eyes are better than anyone I can even see your dreams. But its  morning so you have to tell me about your dream. Xin-ye told him everything. How a creepy woman runs towards her. Holding someone's head covered in blood Harry : Xin-ye I don't want to scare you but. It's not normal I think someone has captured your dreams. Xin-ye ( scared ) : whatttt. How can someone do this?? Harry : I am not sure. But it can be a Demon or Xin-ye : Or whatttt Harry : I think we should ask Lu Jing's help because if it's not a demon. It can even kill you Xin-ye is getting more and more scared : do you really think that he will help me.

Harry : He will help us. Because he wants your help Lin who was just passing from there heard everything Lin : I will also help you.

Xin-ye : ahhh you scared me. When did you come here? Lin : Xin-ye I think we should tell everything to mom and dad. Xin-ye :

I don't think we should tell them anything right now. They will get more scared and worried.

Lin : ahhh ok then I am going to call that devil ( Bothered ) Lu Jing's mom picked up the call : hello Lin : hello. Is Lu Jing there?Aunt : Lu Jing. No he isn't here I think he has gone to see someone. Lin : ohh ok.. Hangs up.

Xin-ye : ahhhhhhh this devil. where has he gone now.

In Night

Xin-ye and everyone was in her room. Xin-ye : Mom Dad. You both should go to your room and sleep. You both have more works to do. And Lin is here for me. If anything happens then we'll call you. Mom Dad left.

After some hours. Xin-ye & Lin fell asleep. In dreams : That creepy woman started running towards xin-ye. But this time Harry was also there. He was trying his best to stop her. For some time he stopped her but after some time Harry got badly injured. That lady comes near Xin-ye. Xin-ye was looking at Harry who couldn't even move. That lady was about to touch her face. And Xin-ye accepted her fate. She closed her eyes. But suddenly. She opened her eyes and saw something.

That creepy woman disappeared. Lu Jing then goes to Xin-ye.. who is still in shock. Lu Jing : Yaaaaaa come to your senses ( shakes her body ). Xin-ye : huh! how did you get here ? And Harry. They go towards harry. Xin-ye holds Harry and says : We will save you. ( Teary eyes ).

# CHAPTER 14

Xin-ye ( emotional ) : ( holding Harry in her arms ) We will save you. Lu Jing ( looks around ) : We have to get out of here faster or she will come again. My powers are not enough to defeat her because she's a witch. The power of the witch is more powerful at night. I can fight with her, but cannot kill her completely.

Xin-ye ( tensed ) : how do we get out of here? Lu Jing : When you were sleeping, was there anyone in the room besides you two?Xin-ye : ( thinks a little ) yeah. Lin was there. Lu Jing : ask him to wake you up. Xin-ye : how do i tell him to wake me up? while i'm here. Lu Jing ( thinks for a moment ) : Now there's only one way to scare you here? so that you wake up in fear,Xin-ye (take a deep breath): Ok.

Before Lu Jing could do something everyone was already in Xin-ye's room.

Xin-ye ( shocked ) : How did I come back? you didn't even scare me ( Looks at Lin who was sitting beside her). Did you wake me up. Lin : nodded you were sweating. And you were making weird faces like you were shocked. Xin-ye ( happily ) : you did a great job my brother. Lin looks at Harry and Lu Jing. Lin : what happened to harry how did he get injured and what is this devil doing here ( So confused ).

Xin-ye explains everything to Lin.

Xin-ye looks at lu Jing and asks : how did you come in my dream??? Your mother picked up the call when we called you and she didn't know about all this so how did you know ( So many questions ).

Harry was in so much pain Lu Jing uses his powers to cure Harry. Now, harry's condition is better ( all his wounds disappear ). But Suddenly, Lu Ling falls on the floor.

The three of them got shocked.

Xin-ye and lin go closer to him while Harry was trying to stand and walk.

Xin-ye shakes his body but nothing happens. After a while she looks at his hands which have turned dark black.Xin-ye holds his hands and notices that his hand is turning into a stone.

Lin : what is happening ( scared ).He is a devil who is very powerful. Or the most powerful but still he is looking powerless and now he is unconscious.

They all were so confused.

It was already 6 o'clock.

Lu Jing's eyes moved and opened slowly. Xin-ye was sitting beside him. While Lin fell asleep. Xin-ye : how are you feeling now ? Are you ok. Lu Jing tries to sit and notice that his left hand has turned into a stone. Xin-ye : Can you tell me now? Everything. Lu Jing : That witch she wants to kill you. Xin-ye ( a bit nervous ) : I know that. But how did you know that it's a witch? Lu Jing : From the day you were not coming to school. I started feeling some changes inside me. So I came to your house yesterday but at the same time I felt something very strange. And when I came to my senses. I realized that it was night and I was sitting somewhere on the side of the road. Then I started going to my home, but then I saw the moon shining brightly and its light was shining above your house. And the next moment I entered your room and because of that light I reached inside your dreams.

Xin-ye :All of this makes sense, but how did your hand become like this and you fall on the floor suddenly.

Lu Jing : She's a very old witch she does black magic. Xin-ye : ahhhh that bloody witch. What will she get after killing me huh? Lu Jing : I don't know but she doesn't want your necklace.

Suddenly someone knocked on the door. Xin-ye : who is there? Mom : it's me. Open the door. I want to see if you are ok. Xin-ye ( gulped and looks at lu Jing ) : ( in mind : Mom can't see him in my room. Especially not so early in the morning ) : You have to hide ( looks at lu Jing ). Lu Jing : huh!  ( His expression was like what is she going to do. It's her mom who wants to see her. She should open the door. Why is she hiding me).

Xin-ye holds his right hand and pulls him to stand she tells him to hide behind the curtains. Lu Jing was confused. But does as she said.

Xin-ye opens the door. Mom : what took you so long. ( Enter inside the room ) you haven't slept at night. Right ? Xin-ye : I will sleep now ( Smiles ) Mom : Xin-ye. It seems to us that someone has done black magic on you ( xin-ye's face was like - how did she find out ) so today we will go to church to pray for you. Her mom hugs her. Xin-ye fakes a smile: Mom don't think too much I will be fine.

Mom : Why did you close all the curtains, let some sunlight come inside the room ( She walks towards the curtains ). Xin-ye : Mother, I am going to sleep now, so leave it closed otherwise all the lights will disturbed me. Mom : ok.. But now you have to go to school too. Your exams are starting next week ( Tensed ). Xin-ye : hmmm I know.. Mom left.

Lu Jing came out. Lu Jing : why did you hide me? Xin-ye : ummm nothing ( in mind : ahhhh what if my mom misunderstood him or me ). What's the next plan? Lu Jing : First of all we have to find that witch. Xin-ye : And how are we going to do this Mr. Devil. Lu Jing ( looks at her ) : I don't know. Xin-ye : ohhh so we have to find a witch but we don't know how. Wow. We can't do anything to her at night.. Ahhhhhhhhh why did I get that necklace. I wanted to enjoy it but what's happening now is making me.. Arghhhhh.. Lu Jing : I have to go home.. Xin-ye : this time keep your phone with yourself..

Around 12 o'clock xin-ye wakes up. She took a bath and came down to the hall. Xin-ye : mom I am hungry. She started eating food. Mom : xin-ye. Your tutor called me she told me that. She had a minor accident yesterday so. She won't come to our home today. But your exams are coming. So, you have to go to her house. Xin-ye : Ohh.. But mom I don't know her address. Mom : I will forward you her house address. Xin-ye : ( in mind : ahh I don't want to go outside. But she is injured ).

After some times around 2 o'clock Xin-ye was going to her tutor's house. She was using Google map to reach her house. After struggling a little she found her house. She rang the door bell. But nobody opened the door but suddenly the weather started changing.

# CHAPTER 15

Xin-ye rang the door bell. But nobody opened the door but suddenly the weather started changing Xin-ye looks at the sky and then a very strong wind starts blowing Xin-ye's phone rings Xin-ye picked up the call. But her eyes were just looking at the sky. Xin-ye : hello.. Mom : Xin-ye. I forgot to tell you that we have to go to church today so you have to come home by 4 o'clock. Ok..Xin-ye : Mom but weather.

Mom : The weather is good. Don't forget the time ok. Hangs upXin-ye : huh!?? The weather is good?? There is something wrong Xin-ye started calling lu Jing & ringing the bell at the same time. Lu Jing picks up the call. Xin-ye explains him everything & Send him her live location.

Door opens Mei Lien ( tutor ) was standing in front of her Mei Lien's left hand was bandaged. Xin-ye greets her. And looks at the weather which was now back to normal ( In mind : strange ).

Xin-ye goes inside her house. And examine everything & Says : do you live alone?? Mei Lien nodded in yes : Xin-ye you can sit here I have to use the washroom. And went from there.

Xin-ye was just scanning the whole place. And takes out her phone but there was no signal. In just some seconds she heard someone's screamed. She got a bit scared. And thinks. It can be my tutor I should go and check. But what if it's a demon. Arghhhhhhh I am going.

Xin-ye started going in the direction from where those voices were coming. She was scared because the sound was a becoming scary. She reached to a room. The door was locked. When she touched the door knob. The sound/ scream everything stopped. It was like a pin drop silence. It becomes more scary than before. Her hands were shaking.

Xin-ye removed her hand from the door knob and all sounds/screams started again this time she fell on the floor. She started sweating. And was wishing for someone ( lu Jing ) to help her. She started feeling that someone is coming near her her heartbeat was getting more and more fast. She turns around to look but nobody was there. She turn back but nobody was there too. She thought of going back to the place where Mei Lien left her. Xin-ye stands and turns around but this time she saw something that she screamed very loudly she was the same witch who used to come in her dreams. But this time she was way more scarier than in the dream. Xin-ye started panicking when that witch started moving towards her. Xin-ye was going backward. But after some back walks she is attached to the wall she was wishing that lu jing would come from somewhere.

She closed her eyes. That witch was just about to touched her. But a white flashing light came out of nowhere and pushed that witch so hard that she fell on the floor about 6-7 feet away from xin-ye neither was that necklace nor was lu jing. That white light came from xin-ye's body. From her heart. In just a minute that light disappears. And xin-ye falls on the floor with her hand on the side of her heart. Her heart was paining. That witch was lying on the floor. Witch tries to get up. But suddenly a black aura covered around that witch. It was Lu Jing who was using his powers. But his one hand already became a stone so, he cannot hold her for a long time.

Lu Jing ( using his all strength ) : Xin-ye ( Xin-ye looks at him while holding her heart/chest ) Run I can't hold her for a long time ( Screamed )Xin-ye tries to stand. She was feeling so weak that she just stood up and walked 2-3 steps and fell on the floor. Lu Jing was also feeling tired his grip on her started weakening. Witch took her chance and used her aura to make them fall asleep. She snapped her fingers and some glitter spread all over the place.

Lu Jing & Xin-ye both fall into a deep sleep.

IN DREAMS

Xin-ye was standing in the middle of the road ( It was night and quite dark ). Xin-ye starts looking for Lu Jing. But before she could take a step. A sound comes to her ears.

Sound : Do you wanna save him. Or. Yourself. Xin-ye ( she was quite scared and was shaking ): Wh-who are you? And why do yo-you wanna kill us. Sound : Awwwwww.. What a pity you are about to die.. but still questioning me..( Laughs ).. I will tell you but before this you have to choose one. Whom you wanna save. This offer is valid only for 2 minutes. If you can't choose one than I will kill you both. Xin-ye ( in mind : Even if I save myself, she will surely kill me because I am her target from the very beginning, but if I save Lu Jing. He will save me because he needs me. Hmm I should save him ) : I will choose Lu Jing.

Sound : Ok then I will kill him right in front of you. Xin-ye ( shocked ) : wait-what?? You asked me to save one. Myself or Him. And I choosed him. You have to save him. Sound : Why should I listen to you ( scary laugh ).

# Chapter 16

Sound : Why should I listen to you ( scary laugh ). It's my world. My rules. Xin-ye : ( in a taunting way ) so, why did you even bother to ask me. Sound : Aren't you scared of me? How can you talk to me like this ( Angry ) Xin-ye : No. I am not scared of a witch ( Although she was very scared but still was trying to pretend that she is brave ).

Suddenly that creepy woman appears in front of her. Xin-ye's face was expressionless but her heartbeat was way too fast. Xin-ye ( in normal voice without any Stummered ) : what do you want? If you want this necklace. Than take it. You are powerful so, it's easy for you to kill me. That creepy woman was standing near her but wasn't that close: who said that I want that so called necklace ( smirked ). What I want is your H-E-A-R-T ( looks at her chest with a creepy smile ). Xin-ye ( still trying to be brave ) : You want my Heart. Then take it ( After saying this she was like whatttt did I just said. Ohhhh no. What if she really kills me to take my heart. But why does she want my heart??? Ahhhhhhhhhhhhh what do I do now ).

Creepy woman : Sure. ( Laughs ) Xin-ye ( in mind : ahhh shit. Where is this devil. She is even more powerful than Lu Jing and Me. I don't even know about my powers that much. Now, who will save us or maybe it's our last day ).

The witch snaps her fingers and Lu Jing appears lu Jing was standing in the air his left hand had become stone. He was trying to move but couldn't as he was covered with a translucent black layered bubble made by that witch. Xin-ye : ( bothered ) Why can't he do anything and his hand.

Witch started mumbling something and just in second xin-ye's leg started leaving the ground she started going upwards. And the same translucent black layer started covering her. It was like a bubble where lu Jing & Xin-ye were locked. Xin-ye started beating on the walls of that bubble. But that bubble was very strong.

After a while Xin-ye notices that. Lu Jing's Bubble started moving. Xin-ye was trying to talk with him but they can't hear eachothers voice Lu Jing's Bubble started cracking. While that witch was mumbling something. Her eyes were closed but hands were moving she was continuously mumbling something.

Lu Jing's Bubble burst after a few seconds. He started falling he falls on the ground. And suddenly he started feeling that his body is burning.

Lu Jing looks at xin-ye who was inside that bubble. And then he looks at the Witch who was mumbling or she was doing black magic Lu Jing tries to use his powers. But his left hand was turned into a stone which wasn't even moving a bit. His energy level was also very low. But he still tries to use the powers. As he started using his powers xin-ye's bubble started cracking. ( Lu Jing's body was burning from inside. He was in way too much pain ). After few seconds xin-ye's bubble burst and she started falling from the air Lu Jing tries to hold her in air with his powers so that she can land safely.

The witch's eyes open as soon as xin-ye touches the ground. Witch ( very angry ) : how dare you? You spoiled my whole plan. Ahhhhhhhhhhh. You two. Bl**dy f**kers. Now, you both will die. She snaps her fingers. And a very strong wave started blowing.

Xin-ye helds Lu Jing's right hand tightly. She could feel the burning sensation inside his body. Xin-ye ( worried ) : Are you ok? Lu Jing ( in pain ) : we need to get out of here. As soon as possible. The waves were very strong. They both were trying their best. Xin-ye : ( in pain -  screamed my heart  ). Lu Jing : what happened. Xin-ye's grip was loosing from Lu Jing's hand. Her hand was about to lose. But Lu Jing held her hands more tightly than before. Xin-ye : My heart. It's hurting like a hell.  And suddenly that white light appeared again.

But this time the amount of light was more than before and more powerful. Everything stopped. That waves stopped. And the sounds of someone's screams started getting louder & louder.

After a while.

Lu Jing taps on xin-ye's face slightly. Xin-ye opens her eyes. Xin-ye ( slowly opens her eyes and saw lu Jing's face ) : You were burning from the inside. But you still saved me ( Emotional ). Lu Jing : I didn't saved you. You saved both of us. Xin-ye : huh! She looks around and get up. Isn't it Mei Lien's house. But we were in a dark creepy place. And that Witch. Looks at lu Jing's left hand. Your hand. ( Shocked ). You hands are normal. Ahhhhhh i am so confused.

Lu Jing : Do you remember that your heart was hurting like a hell and a white light came out of nowhere. Actually it was inside from you. That light burned that creepy woman/witch. Xin-ye : huhhhhh!? You mean. I killed someone but what was that light and. How arghhhhhhhh it's too scary. And one more thing that Witch wanted my heart but why? Everyone wants this necklace from me but. That witch wanted to get my heart.. arghhhhhhh.

Lu Jing stretching his hands : I don't know. Ahhh my hand is back. I missed you my left hand.

# CHAPTER 17

Lu Jing : I missed you my hand. It feels so comfortable. ( He also uses his powers to check ).

Xin-ye : I used to think that devils are more powerful but here ( Giggles ). Lu Jing : ( rolled his eyes ). I wasn't that powerful in front of her because she was an old witch and I am just a new devil who hasn't killed anyone yet. ( Walks towards her ) ( Highlighting his words ) Do you know what makes the devil become more powerful ( Smirks ) & back off.

Xin-ye : What do you mean? ( A bit of a shock ) Do you have to kill someone to become more powerful.. ahhhhhh.. I can't believe him blindly.

Lu Jing suddenly asks : what were you doing here? Xin-ye : I was here for ( She realise that Mei Lien isn't here ). She started searching for her. Lu Jing : What are you looking for now. Xin-ye : I was here for my tuitions. And my tutor I think she was also hypnotised by that witch. ( She suddenly stopped searching ). Or maybe she was the WITCH.. ahhhhh no-no-no how can she be a witch.

Lu Jing : ( looks around ) She was the Witch. Look at this room. There is no mirror. Witches don't use mirrors because in mirrors their real appearance reflects.

Xin-ye : you know too much about all this. ( It was a compliment with a weird face ). Lu Jing : Let's go now.

It was already 3:45.

At home.

Mom : You came earlier. Xin-ye : hmm mom. Tutor said that she won't be able to teach me. Because she is going to her hometown tonight. Mom ( a bit worried ) : Ohh.. But your exams are coming and now, we have to find a new tutor for you.. Arghh no worries I will find someone. Xin-ye nodded.

Dad : xin-ye you are back. Good now let's go. Xin-ye : Where are we going dad? Mom : did you forget that we have to go to church today. Let's go.

[ Harry was weak so, Lin was taking care of him at home..... So only xin-ye and her parents went to the church ]

In church. Father did some rituals.

Xin-ye and her parents were about to leave the church. But an old father stops them and ask xin-ye to come with him.

That old father gives her a book ( neither thick nor thin ). And says : You will find your all answers here. Whispers in her ear. It's better than that letter ( Smiles ). Xin-ye was quite shocked & confused too. She touches her necklace. Father : Don't worry. God has choosen you. You must be a precious one ( Smiles and leaves ).

At home.

Xin-ye tells everything to Lin & Harry that happened Today. And Lin & Harry were listening to her very quietly. And were also very interested in all these things. Lin : ( without thinking anything he says ) When will you die? Xin-ye gives him a deadly stare. Her posture changes into a fighter. She was about to punch him. Lin : sorry sorry sorry sorry sorry it slipped out of my mouth ( Leaning his body ). But xin-ye still punched him on his back.

After a while. Xin-ye showed him the book that an old Father gave her. Lin : Let's open it ( Before they can open the book and take a look. A voice entered to their ears ). Mom ( shouts ) : xin-ye... Lin. Come and have your dinner.

After Dinner. Everyone went to sleep. Xin-ye & Lin forget about that book. Xin-ye cuddles Harry as he is sick and sleeps.

Next Morning.

Mom : xin-ye did you have good dreams? Xin-ye : Yeah mom. Mom : we should have gone to church earlier ( She was giving all credit to God & church).

After 4 days Xin-ye is going to school. She is nervous.

In school

Xin-ye was waiting for Ximi. She was very angry on her because she is her best friend. But she didn't even call her and came to visit her. When she wasn't coming to school.

After a few minutes Ximi entered the classroom. She looked. at xin-ye but ignored her. And sits on her seat.

Ximi's POV : -

Ximi was ghost sick from a few days. She was even hospitalized for 2 days. She also wasn't coming to school. And she was angry on xin-ye for the same reason. <Besties mind>.

They both looked at each other and ignored. They wanted to talk but were angry too. They both Don't have any idea that they both were absent from the same day and came to school on same day.

After few minutes. Some girls asks both of them: Were you both really sick? or both of you had gone somewhere else.. Huh!??

After hearing this they both look at each other. Xin-ye & Ximi at the same time : You were sick. A bit emotional & worried too. During lunch break.

They both talked a lot both of them were very happy. In all this conversation xin-ye accidentally tells Ximi about Harry. Ximi : Today I will come to your house to meet that cat. I am very excited ( Xin-ye regreted for a while. But she knew that Ximi will never do anything which will harm. Xin-ye wanted to tell her everything but for this she have to ask Lu Jing & Lin ).

In Library.

Lu Jing gives a book to Xin-ye ( Everyone saw that and started gossiping about them ) Ximi : Yaaa xin-ye are you hiding something from me ( teasing+ suspicious ) Xin-ye : Aishhhhh it's nothing like that.

Xin-ye opens the book. In that book there were so many things about witches and demons ( In mind : ohhh so from here he knew about them ).

Gossips about Xin-ye & Lu Jing started getting everyone's attention in the class. Some girls even started bullying her. But Xin-ye isn't a weak girl. She is like -- I don't hurt anyone or argue with anyone until they start it. If you mess with me, you will definitely regret it.

# CHAPTER 18

Some girls started taunting xin-ye. But Xin-ye ignored it as she wasn't even interested in their so-called gossip.

After School

Xin-ye & Lin reached home. Nobody was there at home.

After few hour. The door bell rings. Xin-ye goes to open the door a person entered inside the house and hugs xin-ye. It was Ximi. They were very happy.

Ximi : Xin-ye ( Excited ) introduce me to that cat. Xin-ye : ummmmm let's go to my room then. As soon as Ximi enters the room Harry starts attacking her. And meowing.

Xin-ye whisper : Harry. She is my friend. Not an enemy ( with a weird smile ).

Harry stops meowing & attacking her. Ximi got a bit scared but still she wanted to touch the fur of Harry.

Ximi reaches out her hand to touch him but Harry starts staring at her. So, she doesn't dare to touch him. And get's a bit upset.

It was an awkward moment for three of them. Xin-ye doesn't want it to go like this so, she takes harry in her arms. And asks Ximi to touch him gently.

Xin-ye makes Harry feel comfortable so he won't harm Ximi. Or scares her.

After a while Lin comes inside the room and asks them : Wanna come with me and my friends?? Ximi & Xin-ye : Where?? Lin ( smirks ) : To the park.

In Park.

They played so many games Harry also went with them. He started getting comfortable with them. And enjoyed everything.

After 3 hours.

It was already 7 o'clock. Ximi : Xin-ye I have to go I just got a call from my parents. Lin ( running towards xin-ye ) : xin-ye ( Breathes ) mom ( while breathing ) mom. Xin-ye : breathe first. Lin : Mom has found a tutor for you and he is waiting for you at home. Xin-ye ( shocked+upset ) : whattt.. Arghhhhh I just got rid of that witch and now.. AhhhhhhhXimi ( confused ) : huh!!!?? Witch? Xin-ye ( nervously ) : I-I mean my previous tutor. She looks like a witch ( Fake smile ). Ximi : ohh.. all the best for the exam. Take care. Bye. Xin-ye : All the best. Bye.

Xin-ye : ahhhhhhh now, I have to study.. Arghhhhhh..

They said good bye to everyone. And started going back to their house.

They were very tired xin-ye & Lin both of them were fighting, talking, teasing each other all the way to home Harry was just enjoying everything because it was funny for him.

They reached the house. Opens the door and run towards the kitchen.

Xin-ye was faster than Lin ( Lin was carrying Harry in his hands) She entered inside the kitchen opens the Fridge and starts drinking water. Meanwhile Lin was standing in the hall like a statue.

Xin-ye was peacefully drinking the water. Mom : You both have no manners. At least greet the aunt/ my friend ( In mind : these two will never behave themselves ).

Lin greets aunt. And was looking at the boy. Who was sitting beside her. Xin-ye comes back to the hall with a water bottle in her hand. She passes the bottle to Lin. Harry : Meowwwww meowwwww. Xin-ye : Huh?? She looks towards her mom. Who was staring her. She noticed that there is an aunt. So, she immediately greets her. Her eyes move further. And her expression changes.

Xin-ye ( gulped ) : Lu Jing. Aunt : Do you know eachother? Mom : Do they??? Xin-ye ( blinking her eyes rapidly ) : He-he is my classmate. Lu Jing : And Deskmate too ( Smiles ). Mom & Aunt : It's even better. Xin-ye & Lin ( they both were like- what's going on here ). Mom : From today onwards he will be your tutor. And as you said that he is your deskmate too so, he can also help you in school. Xin-ye ( she wanted to reject it but can't reject it directly ) : But mom. He also need to handle his own studies. And I can manage on my own too. Or Lin can help me ( Looks at Lin ).

Mom : Lin will you tutor her?? ( She knew that he won't because of the past).

A small flashbackThere was a time when xin-ye's mom decided that Lin will help Xin-ye in her studies. Lin and Xin-ye both agreed on this. On the first day. When Lin was trying to teach xin-ye some topics. But Xin-ye wasn't understanding it. Xin-ye started beating Lin because she wasn't getting that topic & was getting more & more angry, frustrated. So, she started taking out all her frustration on Lin. Lin started crying and went to her mom. And hides behind her. Mom : what happened?? Lin ( crying ) : mom Xin-ye, she is beating/ punching me because-because she does not understand that simple topic. Xin-ye ( she came towards her mom carrying some books, geometry box in her hands ) : mom where is your son. He said he will teach me. But he run away. Flashback over.

Lin : No No No. mom. Please no. I won't help her in studies ( Whisper ) I don't believe her. What if she.. no no no... I won't. Xin-ye ( stares at him ) Mom : stop it. And as far as Lu Jing's studies are concerned he will do his revisions while teaching you. Aunt : hmm.. Don't worry about him. He is good in studies. He will surely help you. Xin-ye : but mom. Mom : Your exams are starting from Monday. Start studying ( looks at Lu Jing and smiles ) Xin-ye take Lu Jing to your room ( A bit rude ) And Lin you also.

Lu Jing, xin-ye, Lin & Harry. They all go to her room.

In room. Firstly Xin-ye punches Lin's back. Xin-ye : You. Now you tell me to help you, I will also say no no mom, I will not. No no I won't ( mimicring of Lin ). My so-called brother.

Lin : so why don't you study properly ( Taunting her ).

Xin-ye : ( deadly stare to Lin ) you. Then looks at lu Jing ( Who was roaming around her room ). Lu Jing : I have come here before but didn't notice your room - it's so messy.. Ewwww..

Xin-ye : It's messy right ( Lu Jing nodded ). Then why are you still here. Go and tell your mom. That you are not interested in tutoring me. Lu Jing ( sits on her bed -- feeling comfortable ) : Looks at xin-ye while smiling. Who said that I am not interested in tutoring you. By the way. Your bed is so comfortable. Xin-ye : arghhhhhhhh ( Calm herself ). Don't you think you are wasting your time here. Lu Jing : No.. I am not ( Smile )Xin-ye : Your smile. It's not giving me a good vibe. What's in your mind. Lu Jing : There is nothing. I just want to help you. As you are helping me I am just doing a favour for you. That's all. Xin-ye : ( rolling her eyes ) ( politely )Mr devil I don't want your help. Or any favour. Lu Jing : ohhhh.. I will leave if your mother asks me to. <swag>Xin-ye : arghhhhhhhhhhh.

# CHAPTER 19

Xin-ye : Arghhhhhhhh ( in mind : what the hell ). Lu Jing : Shall we start ( With a smile ). Xin-ye  : ( Weird face + fake smile ). Yeah.

Lu Jing started teaching her Some topics. Xin-ye ( in mind : woahhh I can understand this. It's so easy. But why do teachers always make it complicated. Looks at Lu Jing who was focusing on teaching her. He is not bad as a tutor. But still I don't want him to be my tutor ) Lu Jing ( looks at her face ) : Focus on the topic otherwise you will failed the exam.Xin-ye : I have never failed any exam ( Looks away ). Lin ( he was also studying/ self-studying there <In low voice> You always escape from failing the exam by 1-2 marks and yet you are so proud.. Wowwww.. My sister's talent.. ( Giggles )Xin-ye ( stares him ).

After some hours.

Xin-ye : ( checks the time ) Don't you think it's too late. You should go back to your house. Lu Jing ( smirked ) : nodded in no I am staying here. Xin-ye & Lin : Whattttt ( Harry who was taking a nap.. Wakes up.. ) Harry ( sleepy voice ) : What's going on here?Are you guys not studying anymore <yawning> Meowwww. Lin & Xin-ye ( at the same time stands & says ) : You are staying here? Harry : Huh?! <Surprised reaction> Lu Jing : If you don't believe me then ask your mom.

Lin & Xin-ye they goes down stairs.

Lin & Xin-ye : Mommmmm..Mom ( mom & Aunt was cooking inside the kitchen ) : What happened. Why are you screaming like this? Xin-ye : Mom will that lu jing be living here? Mom : Nodded… Hmmm…. He will live with us. For 2-3 days. Xin-ye & Lin ( shocked ) : 2-3 days.

Aunt : Are you guys unhappy with this? Xin-ye & Lin : no no no.. We are very happy.. ( Fake happiness ).

Xin-ye ( helping her mom in moving dishes from the kitchen to the dining table) : Mom. But why. Mom : They have just shifted to our neighborhood. And there are still some works to be done in their new house. So, I just offered them to live with us. Xin-ye : Arghhhh. Mom : Go and ask Lu Jing to come and have dinner with us.

At the Dinning table Lin & xin-ye get to know that Aunt & Mom are college friends. Aunt have just shifted in their neighborhood. Aunt : You two are so cute you both must have to come to my house I will feed you many new dishes. Lin & Xin-ye : nodded.

After Dinner ( Lu Jing and Aunt sleep in the guest room )
NEXT DAY
It was Sunday. Timing around : 10 o'clock. Xin-ye wakes up ( sleepy ). She was thirsty. She goes to the kitchen with half eyes closed.

In kitchen. Xin-ye : Lin. Pass me some water. She drinks the water and spit out. Xin-ye : aishhhh… You spoiled brat I asked you ( she was fully awake now ). And noticed that it wasn't Lin but Lu Jing. Lu Jing : What did you just said. Xin-ye : What are you doing here. ( Remembers everything that he is staying with them for 2-3 days ). Aishhhhh.. ( Whisper : I asked for water but he gave me boiled water.. What the f**k ).

Lu Jing : I think you are awake now. Xin-ye ( annoyed ) : So what. And left.

After few hours. They studied. And played a bit.

On Monday. They go to school.

In classroom.

Ximi : Yeah. My babe. How's your preparation. Xin-ye : Not bad but not good too. But I don't care. Ximi : ohhhh.. but you'll still pass I know ( smiled ).

After an hour their exam started.

( This whole week they had exams. Lu Jing taught her for the whole week ).

After a week. Xin-ye : Today is the last exam. Finally it will end. Ximi : Hmmm.. it will end but only for now. All the best.

After exam.

At home.

Mom : How was your exams. Xin-ye : Momm.. Don't ask me about this. Lin : Mine was too good. Xin-ye : passed a weird smile to Lin. Mom : Xin-ye. When will you take your studies seriously. This stupid brat. One more thing. Lu Jing's Mom has invited us.. For dinner so, please behave yourself in their house.. ok. Lin ( happily ) : ok. Xin-ye just passed a sign ok.

Xin-ye goes to her room. And noticed that Harry is not in her room. Xin-ye came back to the hall. Xin-ye : Mom.. Where is Harry? ( Worried ). Mom : huh.... He must be here and there. Look carefully.

Xin-ye : Mom... Are you going somewhere.. Mom ( in a hurry ) : hmmm.. I have to go somewhere urgently. Make sure you two eat food at Lu Jing's house. And apologize on behalf of me ok. Xin-ye : nodded.

Her mom left.

Xin-ye again started searching for Harry. But couldn't find him. Lin : why haven't you changed ( school uniform ) yet. And what are you looking for. Xin-ye : Harry I can't find him anywhere. Look for him with me.

It's been 2 Hours.

Lin : We should ask that Devil. He will surely find him. Xin-ye calls him. Few minutes later. Lu Jing comes to their house.

Xin-ye : Can you use your powers and look for Harry. Please Lu Jing ( in mind : She has never requested like this ) : Let me try to find him. Lu Jing closed his eyes. And started searching for Harry after a while he found him. Lu Jing : someone has imprisoned him. Xin-ye : huh? Imprisoned. But he is such a little cute cat. How can someone. Lu Jing ( in mind : cute.. Little cat has she forgotten that he is a demon. And can kill her in just seconds ). It's a demon catcher. Lin : What? What catcher.

Lu Jing : Demon catcher Demon catchers usually imprisoned/ captured. Demons for their own benefits. Xin-ye & Lin ( they were way too confused ). Lu Jing : I don't have much knowledge of them. But i had read it somewhere. Xin-ye : where? Lin : Do these Kinds of books exist in real life. I can't believe. Xin-ye : A devil is standing right in front of you. If it's real. Then that book's existence is nothing.

Xin-ye : Where is that book. Lu Jing : I don't know. Xin-ye : Then where is Harry?? Lu Jing : I don't know. Lin : Then.. how do you know that someone has imprisoned him. Lu Jing : ( he started at Lin ). We have to find that book.

# CHAPTER 20

Lu Jing : We have to find that book. Xin-ye : But from where did you get that book and where is it right now? Lu Jing : Don't know I will try to find that book in my room. But right now my whole room is very messy because of shifting. Xin-ye : Are you sure that we can find it in your room? Lu Jing : hopefully yes.

Xin-ye ( looks at Lin ) : Then we will help you in finding that book. Lin : Why do I have to find that book with you guys. Xin-ye ( stares Lin ) : He is coming with us ( Fake smile to Lin ). Lin : But. Xin-ye : Let's go to your room.

At Lu Jing's house

Firstly Xin-ye & Lin both greet Lu Jing's Mom. Then they go to Lu Jing's room. His room was way too messy. Xin-ye : This room is messier than mine. Ashhhh it's will take too much time. They started looking for that book and at the same time were keeping everything on its right place.

Lin : Arghhhhhhh.. Why are we doing this. Just to find that Cat I am not finding it anymore ( Sits on the bed + tired ). Xin-ye : Keep your freaking mouth shut. Or else be ready to get beaten by me. And start finding that book. I wish that demon catcher had imprisoned you instead of Harry I would be very grateful. Lin : ( makes weird faces ). Lu Jing was enjoying because his plan was something else.

After some hours around 8 o'clock they cleaned the entire room and had everything set in its place. Lin ( angry + Tired ) : Ahhhh-hhhhh where is that book ( glares at Lu Jing ). Moves towards him.. Yahhhhhhh Is there any book like you mentioned before? Lu Jing ( gulped ) : To be honest. Xin-ye also started looking at him with a tired face : please continue I am hearing.

Lu Jing ( straight face ) : Actually ( takes a pillow in his hand ). That book. Or anything about that demon catcher. Doesn't exist in reality. ( Covers his face with that pillow ). And a little smiling reflection comes on his face. Lin : What you do you mean. Xin-ye's eyes widened : What? are smiling behind that pillow. Wait did you lied to us. Just because you wanted to clean this room.. Arghhhh-hhhhhhhh.. I will kill you. You Bloody Devil Lin & Xin-ye looks at each other and took a pillow from the bed and started fighting.

Xin-ye & Lin was attacking on Lu Jing. While Lu Jing was protecting himself.

After a while. Xin-ye : Stop it. That means Harry hasn't imprisoned by any demon catcher ( Looks at Lu Jing ) then where is he? Lu Jing : Do you really think that I have the power to find someone ( smirked ).( Innocently ) He must have gone somewhere. He will surely come back and he is a Demon, he protects himself much better than you.

Lin ( grinding teeth ) : Harry ( Disappointed smirked ) just because of him. I had to do this whole work. Attacks on xin-ye with the pillow. ( Xin-ye was sitting on the edge of the bed. As soon as

Lin attacked on her. She fell on the floor ). Xin-ye : Arghhhhhh.. You two. Then their Pillow fight starts again.

Someone knocks on the door. Three of them stared at the door. Aunt : Kids lets have dinner first.

Three of them ( Looks at eachother ) : Yeahh.. We are coming.

At the Dinning table. Xin-ye was staring at Lu Jing as if she would eat him. While Lu Jing was trying to avoid those stares.

After Dinner

Xin-ye ( whispers in his ears ) : I won't forget what you did today. And if you ever tried to be oversmart with us. Then be ready.

At Xin-ye's house.

Xin-ye quickly entered inside the house while Lin was tired so he was walking behind her ( walking like a patient )Xin-ye ( shouted ) : Thiefffffffff. Lin ( ran faster and entered inside the house ): Where is thief? Xin-ye : There ( pointing towards the couch ). A boy was sitting on the couch. And was looking at the two of them Lin ( looks at the couch ) : he doesn't look like a thief is he your classmate Who are you? Xin-ye : ( taunting ) Ask as if he will tell you everything.

Boy : Xin-ye( Come towards them ). Don't you remember me? Lin : stands in front of Xin-ye and says. Stay away from her. Xin-ye : Look. We don't have anything. We are just students. Boy : Ohh shit i didn't realise that I am in human form. ( A big smile was shining on his face ). Lin & Xin-ye ( confused but scared after hearing this ) : what do you m-mean by saying "human form".

That boy converts into a cat. Xin-ye & Lin both of their mouths were open and was scared to death. They both turned and started running outside the house.

Xin-ye & Lin were very scared and started running. They just have taken few steps. And bump into Lu Jing. Lu Jing : What are you doing. Isn't your house there. ( Pointing at their house ).

Xin-ye grabs his hand and started running while holding his hand. Lin was also running with them. Lu Jing : Yahhhh.. Where are we going. Xin-ye : Someone is their at our house. Let's go to your house. Lin : hmmm it's better.

Lu Jing Suddenly stopped running and xin-ye was about to fall on road because she was running while holding Lu Jing's hand. Lu Jing pulls her towards himself.. so, that she won't t fall but her head hits on his chin. Lu Jing : aishhhhhh.. Helping you is like finding a new trouble for myself.

Lin : What happened now. Lu Jing : Tell me what's going on. Xin-ye ( pulls him so that he can run but he didn't even move a bit.. Instead he stopped her ) : What do you think you are. That person turned into a cat. Now run ( pulls him ). If you are not coming then I am going ( Leaves his hand ). What if he tried to kill us. Lu Jing : ( grab her hand ) Come with me. Lin : Go wherever you want to I am not coming with you two. Xin-ye : ( released her hand ) I won't go either. Lu Jing ( rolled his eyes ) : Don't forget I am devil I can protect you both. Lin : Yeah.. I forgot that he is a Devil..<disappointed smirked> Where is my life have stucked Devil, demon and my own twin sister is that so called guardian.

Lu Jing : shall we go now. Xin-ye shook her head in no : Ok fine, but you have to go inside first. We will wait for you outside.......o k.....Lu Jing nodded : ok.

Lin ( scared ) : we don't have to go anywhere. He has come here on his own.Xin-ye turned and got scared to see that boy. She quickly went behind Lu Jing. Lu Jing covers xin-ye.

Boy : ( politely ) Xin-ye. Don't be scared I won't harm you. Xin-ye : how did he get to know my name he must have came here to get this necklace ( touches her necklace ). Or maybe he have hidden Harry. Lu Jing : who are you Boy : I am Harry Mr Devil ( Demon smirked ).

Lin : huh? H-A-R-R-Y. The boy/Harry turned into a cat. And stands beside xin-ye. Xin-ye bent down and looks at him carefully. Lu Jing : looks at xin-ye do you wanna die. That you are looking at him like this.

Xin-ye : ( eyes on the cat ) He looks like Harry. But Harry can't convert into a human. Can he? Harry : Of course I can I am demon. After 7 years of being an animal. We convert ourselves in human forms so, that we can get along with them. Because animals life span isn't that long. Lin : You mean. That. The boy is your human form Harry convert himself into that boy. Xin-ye : Don't give shocks to us. Just be in one form Harry ( smile+shy ) : ummm actually I just got this face today. So I am very happy & excited.

Xin-ye ( whispers in Lu Jing's ear ) : Is he really Harry? Lu Jing ( Annoyed ) : I don't know? Harry : Xin-ye. You can ask me some questions to confirm if I am Harry or someone else. Xin-ye : huh? Oohh.. ( In mind : What should I ask him ) what happened with me recently? Harry : Are you asking about that Witch? Xin-ye ( expressionless ) asks some more questions and Harry answers them correctly. Lu Jing : I don't think we should discuss this on the road. Xin-ye : hmmmm let's go home first.

At home

Lin : Even if you are Harry. We can't keep a boy in our house. And we have no idea what you will do Harry : I haven't harm anyone yet. And I won't do it in future too. Xin-ye hits on Lin's head. Don't forget that he has also saved me from that witch. Lin : Now, I can't say anything. But he can't stay here. Xin-ye : So, where do you think he will go. Lin : arghhhhhhh.. Firstly I don't understand why you want you to keep this demon. And secondly.. I don't have any idea.

Harry : Don't worry about that I won't bother you guys I have found a place for me & I will move there tomorrow. Xin-ye : huhhh?! You found a place to live Harry ( smiles ) : yeahh.. Today I went to find a place so, you won't feel uncomfortable around me. And I have found a place near this neighborhood.

Lin ( looks at Xin-ye aggressively ) : He went to find a place ( looks at Lu Jing ) Nobody had imprisoned him.

Harry : Imprisoned? Xin-ye : Nothing. So, you will live somewhere else. Alone?? Harry nodded.

Lu Jing : between whom am I stuck. Their so-called drama.. Arghhh..Xin-ye : Don't forget what drama you played today just for cleaning your house. You could have done with your powers too couldn't you? Lu Jing : Didn't you volunteer yourself. Xin-ye : My bad. But from today onwards I am not going to believe you.

Lu Jing : As you wish.

Lin ( suspiciously & suddenly ) : Where were you going at this hour?? Lu Jing : I had come here to throw the garbage and was on my way home when you guys met me. Lin : ohh.. That makes sense.

Lu Jing ( fake smile ) : Is there anything else you want me to do. Xin-ye : No. You can go. Lu Jing ( annoyed ) : Thank you and left from there.

# CHAPTER 21

**N**EXT DAY

In school

Teacher entered the classroom. Everyone one : Good morning Mam.

Teacher : Students. Today we have a new student. Everyone ( gossiping ) : mid year admission? Teacher : let me introduce you to your new classmate. Come in.

Harry entered the classroom Harry ( huge smile ) : Hello every-one I am Harry ( Looks at xin-ye ) I am your new classmate. As you all know that I have taken admission in the mid year of the session. So, I hope you guys will help me in studies and in other activities. Thank you.

Everyone was happy with his nature.And his looks were also great. Classmates : He is so good looking. And he isn't cold like Lu Jing.

Teacher : You can sit on that empty Desk. [ That desk wasn't very far from Xin-ye but also wasn't that close ]They both look at each other and smile.

Teacher : So, I have one more important announcement. Today , I have got your exams result. So, who ever have scored less than 50% in their exams have to come with me. To my office.. Ok.

Everyone nodded.

Xin-ye : What the f**k. Ahhhhhh I am done now. Ximi ( worried ) : Xin-ye. All the best.

Teacher started giving them their results.

Xin-ye started calculating her marks. Xin-ye ( happy + shocked ). Truns back ( Ximi sits behind her ). Xin-ye ( surprised + happy ) : Ximi. I have scored 53% in total. Ximi ( shocked ) : Are you sure. Give me your report card I will calculate it.

Ximi calculates it ( Shocked + surprised ) : what. It's like impossible one. You have literally scored 53%. Woah. Xin-ye ( proud on herself ) Ximi : That means your new tutor is really something. Xin-ye ( all her happiness disappears ) turns back. Looks at Lu Jing ( In mind : Why the f**k I scored more than 50% Arghhhhh.. if mom will know it. She will surely give all the compliments to him. And will force me to study with him )Head down with a down face.

Lu Jing : Didn't you scored 53%. Then why are you behaving like you have failed the exams .Xin-ye ( stares him. Makes faces and look down ). Tapping her legs on the ground. Lu Jing : Childish. Leave it. Xin-ye : What's your score. Lu Jing : 94%. Any problem.

Xin-ye : Aishhhhh.. Why did he score that much I don't want to be tutored by him. Nahhhhhhh.

At Lunchtime

Harry came to Xin-ye desk : What happened to you. Ximi : Do you know eachother? Xin-ye ( nodded ) : hmm... I know him. Ximi : Then why don't I know him. Is he your. Xin-ye : Aishhhh.. Stop your nonsense I just know him. And you have already met him.

Ximi: huh? I have met him ( looks at Harry ) Harry feels a little uncomfortable with her stares. Xin-ye : I-I mean. You have met him today haven't you. Ximi : ohh.. extending hand for handshake. Hey I am Ximi ( Smiles )Harry : Handshakes I am Harry ( awkward smile ). They had their Lunch in Canteen. Lu Jing doesn't have lunch with them.

After 2 periods of studying they had sports period.

Everyone went to the ground. The Sport Teacher was absent today. So, everyone can do/play whatever they want.

A group of boys and Harry asked Xin-ye to join them in basketball. Xin-ye : Not bad.. Bro you have already made some new friends Harry : Are you joining us or not? Xin-ye : of course I am joining you guys.

Ximi ( cute face ): what about me? Xin-ye ( cutely ) : Awwww.. Let me Just play with them for 15 minutes. Please. Ximi : oh.. Ok.. But only for 15 minutes after that you have to play with me. Xin-ye ( eye wink with a ok sign).

They started playing basketball. Boys : You are really very good at basketball. Why don't you join basketball club. Xin-ye : I am not allowed to join it. Because of my grades ( Fake smile ). Now I have to go as my friend is waiting for me.

Harry gives her a water bottle : You were really amazing. Xin-ye : thank you Mr demon. By the way. How did you learn playing basketball. Harry : demon skills ( Eye wink ) and left from there.

Ximi who was watching her. Xin-ye : Let's play badminton. Ximi : what were you talking with him.. Huh? Xin-ye : casual talk. Let's play now. Or else the period will over soon. Ximi & xin-ye started playing. But all of a sudden. Xin-ye felt a sharp pain in her heart but didn't let Ximi know that.

Classmate : Ximi. Principal mam is calling you. Ximi : oh.. Ok. Xin-ye : Go. I will wait for you in the classroom.

Everyone was still on the ground. Xin-ye went inside the classroom sits on her desk. And head down. She was enduring that pain. She thought that it's because she played a lot. Lu Jing came and sits beside her.

Lu Jing ( drinking water ) : What happened to you? <No reply> Weren't you playing with Ximi. Suddenly xin-ye's head fell on Lu Jing's lap. Lu Jing's every actions stopped. He keeps his water bottle on the desk. Lu Jing : I am not your pillow. Wake up. <No movement>. He shook her head. And realised that her body is freezing. Lu Jing : she has healing powers. Then why is she freezing? ( He tried to wake her up ). He splashes water on her. After a few seconds Xin-ye wakes up and finds herself on Lu Jing's laps.

Lu Jing : Will you please sit properly? Xin-ye ( she adjusts herself ) : When did you come here ( A bit awkward ). Lu Jing touches her head when Xin-ye was lost in her thoughts. As soon as he touched her head she looked at him with a confused face. Lu Jing : Your head. It's still cold ( Hold her hand ). Your hands are also freezing. But ( looks at her face ) You look so fine. Xin-ye : huh? Removed her hand from his hands I am totally fine. Then again a sharp pain she felt. She held her chest tightly as if a sword is thrusting into it.

Lu Jing ( a little worried ) : What happened?Xin-ye : It's like someone is thrusting his sword into me. Lu Jing : Sword. Right inside your heart. Xin-ye ( nodded ) Lu Jing ( in a serious tone ) : Hold your necklace.

# CHAPTER 22

Lu Jing ( in a serious tone ) : Hold your necklace. Xin-ye holds her necklace and she starts feeling well. Xin-ye : it worked. But how did you know that it will work. Lu Jing : don't you have powers because of this necklace ( Serious ) And one more thing I am not sure but there is another demon. Xin-ye : huh? Demon But you said that there is only one demon and it's Harry. Then suddenly. Lu Jing : there are some other demons who are way too powerful. They can hide their existence from everyone. And that pain in your heart. Can be made by that demon.

Xin-ye : Aishhh.. Demons again I thought it will be fun. But now it's getting painful.. Ahhhhhh.

After few minutes

Everyone started coming back to the classroom from the ground. Some classmates stares at them. And started their gossips.

Xin-ye & Lu Jing looks at eachother then looks away.

Teacher entered the classroom and started teaching.

Last period bell rings. Everyone started packing their things. Most of the students have left the classroom. There were only

5-6 students. Xin-ye & Ximi were casually talking and some girls started saying blah blah about them. Firstly Xin-ye ignored and started going outside the classroom. But two of them block their way. Xin-ye was getting annoyed with their nonsense. Xin-ye : I am warning you. Stop here or else. Girl 1 : what will you do. Will beat me. Girl 2 : ummmmm maybe she will complain to the teacher. But she will be the one in the fault. Ximi ( very angry ) : what's her fault.. Huh! What have she done to make you say these things ( Xin-ye : ignore them. They are just fu**ers ). Girl 1 : Mind your words. Xin-ye : why should I mind my words. You are the one who is creating the scene. Girl 3 : Aren't you the one who is involved in puppy love. Xin-ye : Even if I am. Them what's your problem. Are you jealous that you don't have any so called puppy love. Ximi : of course. They can't even get into a relationship. That's why they are interfering in other's matter. ( Smirks ). Girl 1 : You. Bloody. ( She tries to push Ximi ) but xin-ye twisted her hand. And that girl fell on the ground. Ximi & xin-ye left the classroom and went to their house.

Xin-ye was way too annoyed by the things that happened today. All the things were running inside her mind. Lin ( normally ) : what happened to you. Did someone bully you? ( Smiles ). Xin-ye ( stares him ) Lin : Did someone really bully you. Xin-ye : If you don't want to get beaten by me then shut your mouth Lin ( angry ) : what the I am asking you because I thought I should help you. But your attitude. It's the worst thing you have. If someone had really bullied you then I am grateful to that person as you are the worst.

This line "you are the worst" made her feel very sad. Because these words. She have heard it from almost everyone but today it felt different. It just makes her think that she is good for nothing.

Next Day

In school

Xin-ye was already very upset she wasn't talking to anyone. Ximi was also worried for her. She asked if she is upset because of what happened yesterday in the classroom. Lu Jing heard it but didn't react. Xin-ye didn't say anything.

In lunch break.

A student : Xin-ye. Your class teacher is calling you in the staff room. Ximi : why? Student : I don't know. Ximi : oh-ok..

Xin-ye goes inside the staff room while ximi was standing outside and hearing everything.

Xin-ye looks at those girls who were creating the scene yesterday ( annoyed smirked ) : ( Low voice ) You can't even handle things on your own. Teacher : Did you fight with them. Someone's mother : Look at my daughter's hand. She twisted it. She isn't able to move it. And you are asking if they had fight. Just punish her.

Xin-ye To that lady : Mam I didn't start the fight..... ( She tells them everything that happened yesterday ). Someone's Mother/S.M : so will you break her hand. Xin-ye ( rudely ): I didn't break her hand. She was the one who started the fight and was going to hurt me.. ( She didn't involved ximi's name in all these conversation ). It was just a self defence ( Xin-ye was trying her best not to cross her limits but some of her words were not acceptable to that lady )S.M: don't you have manners. This is how you talk to elders. And how dare you touch my daughter. Teacher : mam please calm down. She is also a student and these things are common between students to have some conflicts.

S.M doesn't listen to the teacher. She came closer and closer to the xin-ye and again asked her : how dare you to hurt my daughter.

Xin-ye was already feeling very upset. And her words were making her go more angry and hurtful... Tears were already in her eyes which she was hiding.. Her whole body was shivering : ( harshly ) Firstly I wasn't the one who started all this bullshit.... And about touching or hurting your so called shameless daughter-I touched her with my hands and before judging me... Please look at your own daughter.

Teacher ( high tone ) : xin-ye. This is how you talk to elders.... Huh?? Go back to your class I will talk to you later.

Xin-ye started going out from the staff room. She knew what she said was wrong. She was biting her lips and blinking her eyes rapidly so that she could control her tears. She came outside the staff room and saw Lin & Ximi. Lin ( angry ) : what was that? Why didn't you tell me all these things. Xin-ye ( controlling herself ) : didn't you say that I am the worst. Now be happy. Now I also get to know that I am worst. And started going from there with a speedy walk.

Ximi : Did you say these words to her. She run towards her but couldn't find her. Lin and Ximi both of them started searching for her. Harry also started searching her after knowing all this. Almost everyone get to know that xin-ye have misbehaved with an elder person.

Meanwhile Xin-ye was sitting on a bench in the playground and trying not to cry. But all the things were making her feel like. She is good for nothing. She is not a good person.

Lu Jing sits beside her ( Not looking at her ) : If you want to cry... You can cry... Xin-ye : You don't have to worry about me I know you are here with me because I am that so called guardian who can make you a human again. Or else you won't even be talking to me like you are. You can go and do your work. You don't have to do things for me. I will still help you because you are the only one whom I can help.

Lu Jing : You are such an overthinker stop thinking nonsense already you don't have any brain cells ( Offers her a cold drink ) Drink it. Xin-ye : I said you don't have to be polite with me. Lu Jing attached that cold drink to her cheeks xin-ye looks at him : You are looking like a tomato What if someone got scared of you.

Xin-ye took the cold drink and started drinking it : You don't have to console me. You can go I will be ok in sometime. Lu Jing ( friendly tone ) : I am not here for you I was just wondering here and there and saw someone crying. Xin-ye : I didn't cry ( a tear falls from her eyes. And she quickly wipes it. Lu Jing : maybe I was wrong.

Lin , Ximi & Harry also come there Ximi hugs xin-ye : I have explained everything to the teacher. Don't worry... There is nothing wrong you did. Harry : If you want to take revenge with them. Just tell me I will help you with my ( He stopped because Ximi was also there ). Xin-ye ( took a deep breath ) : You don't have to do anything I am fine. Lin ( he wasn't making eye contact with xin-ye ) : he offered some chocolates to Xin-ye. Xin-ye ( smile but was still very upset ) : Thank you ( accepted the chocolates ) but I am not going to forgive you. Lin ( smiles ) : ok.

# CHAPTER 23

After the Lunch

Everyone went back to their classes. Xin-ye was a bit upset because of what happened and the only thing that was running in her mind was. She is a mannerless girl..who doesn't know how to talk with elders.

The class teacher entered the classroom. Class teacher ( frustrated ) : Class I am really very disappointed by your behaviour. Now, I don't want anyone to spread any kind of rumours. And if this kind of thing happens again then be ready for a serious punishment. And Xin-ye ( xin-ye stands with an innocent face ).. I know it's not your fault but I have to change your seat.. So please go and sit there ( points at an empty Desk ).

Xin-ye packed her stuff and started going towards that desk.. Teacher : ( Angry ) Xin-ye.. Where are you going? Sit back to your seat..... Faster.....Xin-ye : But....mam....you asked me ( Looks at Lu Jing who was already looking at her ). So, it's you ( She sits back at her previous desk ).

Teacher : ( annoyed ) Why did i come here ? Urghhhhh..... She leaves from there without saying anything.

Xin-ye ( feels better than before ) : That means no-one remembers anything [ a smile appears on her face but as soon as she realizes that she remembers everything her smile fades] Can you erase my memories please? Lu Jing : No.. I can't...... [ The person who knows about him or about his powers.. He can't delete/erase their memories.]Xin-ye : no but why? ( childish face ).( Head down/head on the desk ).

A few days passed.

At school.

Everyone is very excited because today is going to be a very big basketball competition between their school and XY School.

The competition is going to be held in the second half of the school. So, everyone after their lunch gathered in the basketball court to watch the whole competition. Xin-ye was also very excited. But Lu Jing was just neutral.When everyone was in the basketball court Lu Jing was somewhere wondering in the school.

Lu Jing bumped into someone. Lu Jing ( without looking at the person ) : Sorry( Started going ahead ). That boy : Hey bro! ( Mysterious smile ). Lu Jing ( looks at his face and got surprised ) : What the fuc* are you doing here? ( Grabs his neck ) That boy ( smirks ) : Don't forget who I am (Released himself from Lu Jing's grip ) And One more thing ( Whispers in Lu Jing's ears : I know you have found her ).Just wait and watch.( With a mysterious smile he left from there ).

Lu Jing ( a bit tensed ) : What does he want now? And How did he managed to find this place..urghhhhhhh...and where is this stupid xin-ye. He started finding and remembers that she is in the basketball court.

He rushly went to there and saw Xin-ye...Xin-ye was waiting for the starting of the competition. Lu Jing grabbed her hand and asked her to follow him. Xin-ye ( causally ) : Competition is just about to start I am not going anywhere. Lu Jing ( angry ) : Come with me. Xin-ye : I am not your slave. Why do I have to do what you want me to do.. Huh? I said I'm not going anywhere.. Lu Jing saw that boy entering in the basketball court as a XY school team member...He was getting more anxious & angry he didn't want him ( that boy ) to see Xin-ye so he just started walking while holding her hand. They almost left the basketball court. Xin-ye ( angry ) : Are you insane or what. Leave my hand.. Or I will shout.. ( Before she could shout the place changes. They were in the middle of the competition and now they are in a library).

Meanwhile Ximi who went to bring some snacks and drinks for herself and xin-ye came back and started finding Xin-ye. She asked everyone if they know where is she ( Everyone forget what happened just now - Lu Jing's Magic)

In the Library.

Xin-ye ( tried to release her hand but Lu Jing's grip was way too strong ) : ( calms herself down )  What do you want now? huh? What are we doing here? Lu Jing ( put his one hand on her mouth to shut her mouth ) : Shushhh......Stop....Someone is here...Xin-ye bites his hand...Lu Jing ( annoyed ) : Are you a dog?! Why am I even bothering to save you.... I should have handed you to them.

Xin-ye : I am not a thing whom you will hand to someone... Lu Jing  : Can't you see it's a library... And why don't you ever try to understand what I am doing huh? Can't you just listen to me for a while..Xin-ye : Now you are loud...Lu Jing ( annoyed ) : urghhhhh this stupid moron.

( A voice of someone's steps started coming from the another row).

They both looks at each other... And hides behind the bookselves.

After a few seconds the sounds of footsteps stopped..Before they could move.. One bookselve falls on them....Now the situation is like.. Xin-ye is on the floor while lu Jing is top on her  ( lu Jing's one hand on the floor and another one holding that bookselve).

Both of their eyes meets.. Xin-ye was feeling uncomfortable.. She tried to get out of the situation but as soon as she moved a little and Lu Jing's hand slipped from the floor..just for a second their lips met with each other's his whole body was  on xin-ye.

The situation was getting very awkward and uncomfortable for both of them.. Xin-ye : ( with a hesitation ) Use your powers..Lu Jing uses his powers.. Both of them get up...

Both of them were kind a embarrassed and didn't want to talk on that topic. After a little silence.

Lu Jing : Firstly I am really sorry and I brought you here because the basketball court is not safe right now...For you...Xin-ye : Only for me? Is there any Demon..Lu Jing nodded...Xin-ye : oh...How long do I have to hide then? Lu Jing : I don't think you can hide from them.. You just need to protect yourself.

That boy : ( teasing tone ) awwwwww.... What a sweet & caring conversation is going on...Should I wait for a little more.. ( Deep voice ) or should I just take this necklace <smirked>

Xin-ye : You. Aren't you in the XY school basketball team.

That boy : So, you want my introduction. ( Goes near to her ) I am Zheng Yang ( Whispers ) I am a demon.

Lu Jing uses his powers on him to push him at a very far distance ( The whole library was empty only three of them were there.. All the books, bookselves started falling as they started their fight ).

Xin-ye also uses her powers but it doesn't work.. She was feeling useless....As the fight was getting more serious a girl came out of nowhere and smiled like a princess but was giving vibes like an evil.

As soon as Lu Jing saw that girl his blood started boiling. As if she had done something worst to him.

That girl waves at him : Long time no see I hope you haven't forgotten us ( Smiles - which was irritating lu Jing ).

And who is she ( looks at xin-ye ).Your new crush ( Giggles ) Zheng Yang ( wipes his blood coming from his mouth which disappeared in just minutes ) : No-no-no...... I don't think he will ever be able to have a crush on someone after what has happened to him in the past ( laughs ) He is with her only because she is that Necklace guardian...

That girl : Necklace guardian.. This title doesn't suit her.

Xin-ye was confused but angry too. The way they were talking it was quite clear that Lu Jing knows them.

# Chapter 24

That girl ( Name : Suzi ) : Necklace guardian...This title doesn't suit her.....It would be great if you would give it to me ( points at necklace )..( Smirks )Xin-ye : oh really ( Smirked ) then on whom will it suit huh ( folds hand and leans on the desk behind her as if she is ready for the talk war)..Do you think you deserve it.. >>Shook her head in no<<

They both start arguing.. Meanwhile Lu Jing and Zheng Yang thought, the girl fight will start soon.. But that was just a talk fight ( they both were disappointed-especially Zheng Yang ). At this point they were looking frustrated because whenever Zheng Yang says a word either xin-ye or Suzi shut his mouth.

As it was going to start the real fight between xin-ye and Suzi, Lu Jing grabbed Xin-ye's hand and started taking her out.. Saying : Arguing with a useless or shameless person will make her feel tired. As he started dragging her. Suzi grabbed another hand of Xin-ye and stopped her..Suzi : You can go if you want to but she can't...

Lu Jing was already frustrated after seeing her and all the words she was saying were irritating him even her voice.. He released Xin-ye's hand from her's which made Suzi angry...Suzi gave some signals to Zheng Yang to attack Xin-ye. Zheng Yang released a grayish aura from his hand. Which was about to hit Lu Jing but Xin-ye turned back and pushed Lu Jing a little from which the aura didn't touch him..

Lu Jing ( annoyed ) : Aishhh... This bloody...( Before he could complete... he saw something which he didn't expect ).

Xin-ye attacks back on Zheng Yang with a powerful silver auro which was so powerful that Zheng Yang ribs cracked.... which wasn't healing...he tried to stand but couldn't.... the pain he was feeling was expressed on his face.. Suzi got scared because she is a human who is no match for Xin-ye and Lu Jing..So, she immediately went near Zheng Yang and asked him to leave with her but his condition was quite critical.

Xin-ye and Lu Jing left the Library & went to the playground which was empty.

On Xin-ye's face there is a quite satisfied smile and her eyes were stuck on her hands.... She wanted to try that silver aura again. But she doesn't remember how she did at that time. > at that time it just automatically happened < .

Xin-ye : I was so good at that time... My reflex action and that aura.... Ahhhhh I want to try it again so badly. Lu Jing was just silently walking with her.

Xin-ye noticed him and hesitated a little bit but still asked : Umm.... If you don't mind.. Can you tell me about those two people who were there in the library? If you don't want to share it's ok.... it's fine...

[ Note : Lu Jing didn't explain to her in detail he just roughly gave her a review]

Lu Jing : They are the reason of what I am right now. That boy Zheng Yang used to be my best friend and that girl Suzi used to be my crush I know it's weird but it was like that I used to find chances just to talk to her and one day Zheng Yang asked me to confess my feelings and I agreed with him. One day I found my chance after school I tried to talk to her but she just smiled we were just walking and found that we were on the wrong street it was quite an isolated area.. But i didn't think anything I was just finding my chance to confess to her. Later I noticed that her eyes were stuck on a tree I asked her if she wanted a flower from that tree..She nodded with a smile.. her smile always made me feel happy and I decided to pluck that flower. It was quite a beautiful and unique one... I had never seen that flower before and It was also my first time to walk on that street.

The tree was inside the house garden....And the door was locked so, i decided to climb over the walls and pluck some flowers.. As soon as I pluck a flower.. I felt that someone was shaking the tree.... I got scared but wasn't showing it because Suzi was watching me I was trying to pretend that I am all fine.. I plucked more flowers and suddenly I fell on the ground and the rain started..

And ran away from there But the flowers weren't with me...Suzi gets a bit sad and I feel some strange changes in me.. My whole body started itching and weird things were coming in my mind like.. I started having blurr visions and felt like my body and soul are changing everything was quite strange.

At night I wasn't able to sleep because of the changes which were happening... It was painful mentally and physically both.. The next day when I went to school Zheng Yang asked so many questions to me about what happened yesterday and I told him everything even about what happened last night...I didn't know why but I felt that he was feeling quite happy..

A week passed like this and I found so many changes in my dreams and everything was quite scary and related to darkness, devil's demons.... Once again I went to that house because it all started from there......and I stood in front of the tree and started staring at it.....later I noticed that the door wasn't locked this time...... I just entered the house and found a lady covered in black clothes sitting on a table..... Only the back was visible I asked her if I could talk to her but as soon as she turned towards me I got scared to death after seeing her face ( that was a witch ).. It was way too scary I even tried to run away but couldn't.

Later she changed her face with a human face and then I explained what I was experiencing.. Witch was quite understandable she understands all the things she wasn't a bad witch but she doesn't like it if someone touches her things... She told me that she has cursed me and her curse can't be taken back... So, she told me about the necklace guardian... She just told me that only a necklace guardian can solve all these things but it's not going to be an easy task.. She even told me that the necklace guardian is very powerful but his/her life is always surrounded by the demons, witches and other creatures because the Necklace guardian's necklace and heart are the most precious things for them.

Later I found that it was a trap created by my best friend Zheng Yang and Suzi... Because Zheng Yang has been a demon since his birth and Suzi likes him they both just used me to find the necklace guardian... I was broken and was betrayed by my own trusted person I just got separated from them without Letting them know about where I am going...

Xin-ye : Ohh.. Ok... So it means I am very precious. Lu Jing ( shocked because her reaction wasn't expected ) : precious ( an unnoticeable smile appears on his face ) Xin-ye ( takes a deep breath ) : so, what are you planning to do with them? Ummmm should I use this new power of mine on your crush? Lu Jing : ( annoyed stares ) I think I made a mistake... Xin-ye : Tell me..... Should I hurt her or not? But she deserves it.. If I was in your place I would have killed both of them..Lu Jing : Just stay away from them.. I know what I have to do.

As Lu Jing is a devil and very powerful....he steals Zheng Yang's 80% of his powers the powers which he is proud of.. He lost it, although he has 20% of his powers but it's not enough for a demon.. He has basically become a half demon and half human...He can now feel all the pains & can't heal it.

2 MONTHS PASSED

Xin-ye and Lu Jing started working on finding demons and made them do 3 good deeds... They have found many demons... Harry was helping them as he is a cat demon he mostly finds animal demons....Everything was going very smoothly.

# CHAPTER 25

2 MONTHS PASSED

Xin-ye and Lu Jing started working on finding demons and made them do 3 good deeds.. They have found many demons..Harry was helping them as he is a cat demon he mostly finds animal demons...Everything was going very smoothly..

In school

Everyone was gathered in the assembly hall for some lectures....Xin-ye started getting bored and secretly escape from the hall and went to the classroom...Ximi was still there as she is an intelligent student and likes to study.

The classroom was empty.... xin-ye smirks mischievously. She closes the doors. And blocks the view of cameras by using her powers...She started practicing her new powers... as soon as she heard someone's foot steps she opened the door by using her powers sits on a desk( head down ).

A boy enters

The Boy knocks on Xin-ye's desk. Xin-ye looks up with a tired-sick face... Boy : what are you doing here? You should be at the Assembly hall.. Xin-ye ( changes her expression and Smirks ) : ohhh really.... ( Rudely ) Are these all rules only for me huh? What about you... What are you doing here? Mr so called Devil. Lu Jing : I am here to remind you that you can't just use your powers like this ( Fake smile ). It's only going to attract demons & Today I am not interested in involving all this.

Xin-ye : Woahh.... The one who wants me to find demons isn't interested now.... ( Clapps ) All I want is to find all the demons quickly so, that you can leave me alone.. ( In mind : after that I will live and use my powers according to me )...Lu Jing ( side looks ) : ( rudely ) I also don't want to stick with you.

Xin-ye makes an annoying face and starts walking to leave the classroom..As she was walking Lu Jing gave a stare at her and his expression changed...

Lu Jing ( trying to say something but doesn't know how to ) : Yaaa.... ( gulped, rolling eyes ) Xin-ye turns back : ( annoyed ) whatttt? Lu Jing : Y-your....Y-Your.... ( Avoides eye contact ) Xin-ye ( checks herself ) : what mine? Ahhhh say clearly... Or else I am going as you are here. Lu Jing : Your skirt.. There.. There is a stain..... ( Not looking at her ) Xin-ye ( checks her skirt and found, boold stain on her skirt ). Looks at lu Jing who wasn't looking at her.. She feels a bit embarassing and awkward.... ( In mind : why the fu*k it's going like this urghhhhhh...... because of the powers I can't feel the pain and my short term memory, I don't even remember what just happened 5 minutes ago).

Lu Jing also doesn't know what he should do he was confused between if he should leave or stay. Before he could do anything he noticed that Xin-ye had already gone somewhere.

After School.

Xin-ye gets back to her house and gets to know that her Cousin sis is waiting for her in her room..Xin-ye quickly goes to her room.. As soon as she opens her room door she sees her cousin spinning on the spinning chair while reading a book..

Xin-ye : yaaaaa why the hell are you reading the books.....huh hh? Cousin : Yaaa bro.... ( Bright smile on her face ) this book is so amazing...... ( gets up from the chair & Hugs xin-ye ).......Xin-ye : yeahhh.... Your book is amazing as you are paying more attention to this book. Cousin : Bro ( Childish face to get some sympathy ). By the way from where did you get this book. Ahhhhh I am obsessed with this book. Xin-ye ( siting on her bed ) : wait what? It's not yours? Cousin : nodded in no. I found it in your drawer. Xin-ye : impossible... I don't even read books... How am I supposed to read or buy his thick book..Cousin : huh? It's not your book.. Then who's book is this. Anyways it's way too interesting...( Excitedly ) you know what it's about devil and necklace guardian...Xin-ye ( shocked ) : huhhh? Whatttttt? Cousin : what happened.. You know I am really getting curious about another chapter of their life. I wish I had that necklace. Ahhhhh I am literally getting jealous of these fictional characters especially from necklace guardian..

Xin-ye immediately grabs the book from her cousin's hand and starts reading it and finds that whatever is written in the book has already happened to her.

Xin-ye started getting more and more confused and shocked as all the things that are written here have already happened....but how can someone/something knows the inner thought of the person.

After few seconds Xin-ye opens the last page.

At the last page of the book... Everything that happened today was written on the last page....Xin-ye closes the book and starts having negative thoughts like if this book belongs to a Demon or witch.. Cousin : What happened to you ? Huh? Don't tell me that someone died on the last page.......Ahhh I don't want them to have a sad ending..... Let me see if there is a sad ending.. If it's going to have a sad ending then I am not reading the whole book ( sadly ) ( Starts reading and smiles ). Cousin : It's kind of an awkward moment but still I loved this. But why is it ending here?

Xin-ye is still in her thoughts. Cousin : Does it have any 2nd book? Let me check it on social media. Cousin: check the name of the book but there wasn't any name.

Xin-ye saw the front of the book and remembered that this book was given by the father/priest when she went to the church.

Cousin : why doesn't it have any name......... Wait..... bro don't tell me that you are the writer of this book.

Xin-ye ( tries to divert her cousin's mind from the book ) : Yaaaaaa you came here for me or this book.......huh! Cousin : of course for you ( looks at the book )

In the evening when her cousin leaves...Xin-ye started reading the book and found some new things like how to use powers and how it will affect others...Xin-ye started using the techniques which were mentioned in the book.

Lu Jing comes to tutor her...As he entered her room he saw another kind of scenario, many things were floating in the air. Things were moving without anyone's help. Xin-ye's room had become messer than before and quite scary.

Xin-ye ( happily ) : hey look, I have found so many techniques for using my powers in a proper way.... Lu Jing : ohhh ( looks around )

Notices the book. Xin-ye : I didn't know that this book is this much helpful.. Woahhhhhh I want to learn all the techniques as soon as possible... Lu Jing : Tomorrow we have an exam so, it will be better if you will study instead of reading this book.

Xin-ye : it's not a normal book.. You know what... From the day I have this necklace to till now everything that has happened is mentioned in this book... There are also some techniques for demons to use their powers but ( a bit unsatisfied ) those will hurt humans or may kill them.

Lu Jing took the book from xin-ye and started reading it  Xin-ye noticed a chocolate in lu Jing's pocket Xin-ye ( smiles ) : Is this chocolate for me.... Lu Jing ( hesitated ) : no, it's not for you...Xin-ye : oh really. Let me check ( She opens the last page of the book and asks lu Jing to read the last line ).

Last line of the last page...Devil brought chocolate for the necklace guardian as she was on her periods but when she asked if this chocolate is for her devil said-no.

Xin-ye ( teasing tone ) : Are you sure it's not for me? even if it's not for me I am taking this one, you can buy another one for yourself.... ( Smile )

Lu Jing ( in mind : does it also write my thoughts )Xin-ye ( eating chocolate ) : it's quite helpful, right!? But now, you can't hide anything from me ( Laughs ).

Xin-ye was quite happy as she was reading everyone's thoughts and learning new techniques...

Later they studied for some hours and then.. Give their final exams.

Days passed like this and today is the first day of the new semester..

First day of the new class/session

This time Xin-ye, lu Jing and Lin's class's section is same while Ximi and Harry are together but in the different section...The 5 of them were becoming close but somehow Lu Jing wasn't that close yeah but close just as a normal friend.

As it was the first day nothing much happened but it was a good day for everyone except for a new transfered kid.

When Xin-ye, Lin, Harry, Ximi and Lu Jing were going back to there house..They heard some noise. They ignored at first but when they heard someone's sobbing... Lin asked Xin-ye to ignore it but Xin-ye didn't listen to him and went to check if everything is ok or not.

The noise was coming from the narrow street on the left side from where they were... Xin-ye went there and others also followed her as they couldn't leave her alone.

Xin-ye started walking on that narrow street and heard some boys voice...Boys : You bloody fuc**r why didn't you bring more money today? And what did you think huh! That you will live a better life after transferring from the school  ( Laughs ) We will make you pay for it.

Xin-ye : Listen you bloody so called school bullies... Leave him or I will call the cops....Boy 1 ( smirked ) : woahhh. So you have made some friends ( asks the boy whom they were bullying >>the boy was on the floor<< ). Boy 2 started going closer to her : We will leave him but you have to pay for him.. ( Tries to touch her but before he could touch her, Lin punched him on his face ).

Lin started fighting with those bullies.. Then Harry joins Lin and helps him.. As they were fighting, the boy who was on the ground stands and started throwing his stuffs and started screaming...E veryone stopped.

Ximi ( shows her phone's screen ) : I have already called the cops so, it's better for you guys to leave. Or else you know what will happen... ( Smirks ) Bullies left.

Lin ( grabs Xin-ye's hand and asked her to go home or else he will tell everything to mom )..Xin-ye wanted to ask the boy if he is ok or not.. But Lin forcefully took her from there.

# Chapter 26

Lin ( grabs Xin-ye's hand and asked her to go home or else he will tell everything to mom ). Xin-ye wanted to ask the boy if he is ok or not.. But Lin forcefully took her from there.

NEXT DAY

Xin-ye, Lu Jing and Lin were on their way to school in the early morning.... Someone screamed....Xin-ye : Let's go and check what if someone needs our help! Lin ( stops her ) : It can be dangerous...Xin-ye : Yaaa this devil will handle everything... Now let's go and check...Lu Jing ( in mind : huhhh? What is she thinking of me.. A bodyguard... Urghhh ).

The three of them go there and saw the same boys ( bullies ). Bullying the same guy. Xin-ye ( Smirked ) : Again. What do they think of themselves.. Lin : Stop meddling in other's matter. A boy hits that guy with a brick. That guy's head started bleeding.

Xin-ye : what the hell... I can't take it anymore.. ( Starts going towards them ) Lu Jing ( stops her ) : Just stay here and see the magic.. Lin : when did he become this kind hearted ( suspicious expression ).

Lu Jing ( started using his magic and those boys get very scared and ran away from there ).. Meanwhile Xin-ye and Lin were laughing at all this.

Xin-ye ( stops laughing ) : Let's go and help him...Lu Jing ( holds her hand ) : Do you want him to know that all these things or magic was done by you huh?Let's go to school we are already very late.. Xin-ye : His head is bleeding at least give him a first-aid..

Lin : We have done what we should have... And stop being worried for others.. He will be fine... Xin-ye : Ok wait a minute... ( she uses her powers and secretly throws some bandaid on that guy's way.

Lu Jing : What are you going to get in return? HuhXin-ye : I am not doing it just to get something in return..... It's just if I won't help him now then I will regret it for many days that I could have helped him but i didn't do... So I am doing just to satisfy myself.

Lin : why does it only applies on others but not on me huh!?? you have never cared for me this way...Although I am your younger brother ( annoyed ).

At School.

Xin-ye went to meet Ximi & Harry before going to her class... They both talked for some time and then Xin-ye goes to her classroom.

Xin-ye enters in her classroom and sees a girl's bag beside Lu Jing's bag..She feels a bit weird and gets upset for a moment.... She puts her bag on an empty Desk....... And tries to find Lu Jing.

Later Lu Jing comes back with a girl..... And that girl was none other than Suzi ( Lu Jing's ex-crush )..Xin-ye gets way too shocked.. Suzi was wearing the same uniform as Xin-ye.... ( in short she is a new student ).

Lin : ( suspiciously ) Who is she? I have never seen this devil with anyone other than us.....Xin-ye ( annoyed Smirk ) : His crush.......( feels quite hurt from inside but doesn't know the reason...... She wanted to ask many questions but didn't ask anything as it's his life and he can do whatever he wants to).

Lin : huh?! Really? ( Shocked )Lin's friend : Lin Let's go and meet our other friends.. Lin left....

Lu Jing saw Xin-ye Staring at him.. He went towards Xin-ye but Suzi grabs his hand & takes him to his seat.

Xin-ye ( annoyed smile - Closed her eyes and takes a deep breath ) : Ahhhhh this Devil is literally.......And what the f**k is she doing here.

Lu Jing to Suzi ( released his hands from Suzi ) : I have already told you to stay away from me.... I don't care and I'm not even interested to know what you are trying to say to me.... Suzi ( quite frankly ) : Yaaa you were my friend and I don't know anyone here except you so, ofcourse I want to stay with you.. That's why I am sitting with you.

Lu Jing : what!? Sitting with me no way....( Looks away with an annoying face ).

A guy entres in classroom and was looking quite scared. ( The same guy who was getting bullied in the early morning ) Xin-ye notices him.

Guy to Xin-ye ( nervously ) : I am Yi-han c-can I sit here ( he didn't make any eye contact and was just looking down )...There isn't any other empty desk. Xin-ye ( feels bad for him) : Ummm.... Yeah...Lu Jing ( cold voice ) : You can sit on my desk... ( puts his bag next to Xin-ye ).

Yi-han ( nodded ) and went to sit on Lu Jing's desk beside Suzi's.....Suzi felt embarrassed and angry but she doesn't want to show it to others as she doesn't want her reputation to get ruined.

Xin-ye ignores Lu Jing....Lu Jing : why didn't you sit with me. Xin-ye : There wasn't any place for me ( fake smile ).

After few Periods.

Lu Jing : Are you trying to avoid me? Is it because of her ( points at Suzi ). Xin-ye : I am not avoiding you, I am just trying to focus on what the teacher is teaching( fake focused ) Lu Jing ( annoyed ) : urghhhhhh First of all I don't have any idea of her coming to this school..... And secondly..Teacher : Both of you go and stand out of the classroom...Everyone ( looks at them including Suzi ).. Xin-ye : Urghhhhh I didn't even do anything still I have to ahh...

They both went outside the classroom...Xin-ye : Now stop it I am not interested in you and your so called crush/enemy or whatever's stories..Lu Jing : Why are you bringing all these things.... Huh? I have already told you that I don't know what she is doing here..And this morning the Teacher asked me to give her a tour of the school that's why I was with her... That's it.

Xin-ye saw Harry and waves at him..Lu Jing feels a little hurt as she again ignored him.

Harry : What are you guys doing outside the classroom.... Huh?! ( giggles ) Xin-ye : Got punished by the teacher. What about you ?

Harry : I am bunking a class..( Smiles )..Xin-ye : Ohh. What a good thing you are doing bro I am proud of you Harry : I think someone is coming I have to go.... >>Left<<

The environment between Xin-ye and Lu Jing becomes quite awkward as both of them were silent.

After the period get's over...Both of them gets back to their seats...Lin : You got punished with an intelligent student... ( claps ) What a progress my elder sis you have spoiled your deskmate.

Xin-ye gives him a glare.. : Shut up.. Why are we in the same section ahhhhh... I wish I could also get a transfer.

Suzi : Hey Xin-ye.. ( smiles ) Xin-ye looks at Suze : Hey ( fake smile ) ..Suzi : I hope you haven't forgotten me...Xin-ye : ( taunting ) Of course not..... How can I forget someone who uses people just for their own needs..Suze ( suspicious smile ) : I won't let you forget me this soon.. Enjoy your day. ( left ).

Lin : Why do I feel like she is also a demon or one of those who wants this necklace.....Xin-ye : woahhh first time what you are saying is true ( claps )...Lin : What? ( tensed )...( deep breath ) should I talk to mom so that we can get a transfer to another school ( serious tone ) ..( lu Jing's expression changes ).

Xin-ye : huh? are you worried about me? ohhhh my younger brother is worrying about his sister waohhh what a memorable moment..Lin : I am serious...Lu Jing : Do you really think that demons won't be able to find her? If you are worried about your sister that much then stay by her side don't let any stranger get closer to her.

Yi-han ( looking down ) : Ex-excuse me..... can you please give me your notebook I want to complete my pending works...... If you don't want to give me then it's ok...Xin-ye : Take it ( politely+smiles ) Before Yi-han could take the notebook from xin-ye, Lu Jing takes it from her.... And gives Yi-han his own notebook.......Yi-han : huhh!.... Thank you.

Lin : what was that? Lu Jing : He is a stranger to us what if He is a Demon and tried to posses her notebook..Lin : ohhh so this could also happens. Ok ok...Xin-ye : don't know what's going on..

Few days later.

Xin-ye : Ahhhhh.. Why am I thinking about this devil... I don't want to think about him but still... I want to divert my mind from him....Mom ( shouts from the hall ) : Xin-ye I am going to the market don't go anywhere...Xin-ye : Ok mom....Xin-ye : Idea... ( smirks ) ..

Xin-ye goes in the kitchen.. And started searching for some things... Xin-ye to herself : I will try to make a cake..... But I don't even know the C of cake..but No worries, the internet is here to help me  ( laughs on herself ). She started making cake.

Few minutes later... Xin-ye puts the beaker inside the Oven and waits for it to bake properly... ( the whole kitchen has become way too messy...... The flour was spread everywhere even on herself).

Bell rings..Xin-ye..... Her all focus was on her phone she went to open the door while looking at her phone...... She opens the door.......Lu Jing : ( curiously ) What were you doing? Xin-ye ( still focused in phone ) : I was trying to make a cake...... Lu Jing : CAKE! You were making like this ( looks at her from head to toe - giggles ) . Xin-ye : huh!?  Why are you giggling?  She checks herself.. Ohh shit.... Lu Jing ( trying to smell something ) : Where is the kitchen.

Xin-ye : There ( points at kitchen ) But why ...Lu Jing : Your cake is going to blast ( switched off )... Opens the Oven and takes out the beaker.. ( Burning smell spread everywhere). Xin-ye : aishhhhhh why did it get burned.... I did everything which were written here.. Ahhhhhhh.

# CHAPTER 27

**X**in-ye : aishhhhhh why did it get burned.. I did everything which were written here... Ahhhhhhh....Lu Jing : ohh ( looks at her from head to toe and a slight smile appears on his face ).. Xin-ye : Yaaa stop smiling and help me cleaning it. Lu Jing : Why do I have to clean all this with you?  You are the one who made this mess..Xin-ye : ( takes a deep breath ) You are really a devil can't even help someone.. ( A bit rudely )..Lu Jing : Who cares?  And Where is Aunt/your mom. Xin-ye : She isn't at home... ( fake smile ) Now you can go....Lu Jing : I might have to wait for her as my house is locked and the keys are with your mom....Xin-ye : Can't you use your powers and get inside your house ( a bit angry ). Lu Jing : I don't want my mom to doubt on me as the door is locked and I am inside the house... ( Goes towards the couch and sits there looking at Xin-ye ).

Xin-ye ( makes face ) : Really a spoiled devil.... Urghhhh..... she started cleaning the kitchen..Tries to use her powers but it didn't go well vise-versa the things got more complicated.. Lu Jing (

laughs on her situation but didn't want to get noticed by her so, he started playing games on TV ).

Xin-ye : Urghhhhhhh why these powers are not helping me..And this devil, he can't help me but can play games..... What the hell.

Later.

Door bell rings....Xin-ye : Who has come now..... ( cleans herself )...Opens the door....Ximi hugs Xin-ye tightly : Bro I need your help..I think I have made a mista.....( saw lu Jing )Ximi broke the Hug : What is he doing here...... ( confused )....Xin-ye ( explains everything to Ximi ).

Ximi : ohh.. So you guys are neighbours....Xin-ye : Leave him... I have something for you...( goes in the kitchen and brings the cake which she made )...Ximi : What is it? ( touchs the cakes and gives weird looks ). Xin-ye : yaaa don't judge a book by it's cover....Ximi : ok then let me taste it..Xin-ye ( curiously waiting for her reaction ) Ximi ( coughs ) : Xin-ye don't mind but cooking is not for you ( tries to comfort her )..Xin-ye : what do you mean huh? Taste the cake..( coughs )...  Ximi : Drink this water and don't do any experiment with these things ok..... Or we might have to get hospitalized... Xin-ye: Shut up.

Lu Jing ( focused on playing games but was still paying attention to them without letting them know )....

Xin-ye : So now tell me what help do you need? Ximi : Ummm ( signals Xin-ye that she can't tell her infort of Lu Jing )..Xin-ye : Let's go to my room.. But before this I need to hide this cake or else my mom will sent me to the hospital...... But where should throw it.

Mom enters Ximi ( worried ) : Aunty is here..How are you going to hide it now...Xin-ye gives the box of the cake to lu Jing and asks him to throw it in his way back to his home. Lu Jing : huhh? Wait.

Ximi and Xin-ye runs towards her room.

Mom : Xin-ye..Ximi why are you guys running.. These two girls. ( a slight smile ). Notices lu Jing.....Lu Jing greets aunt and hides the cake behind himself... Mom : Ohh so sorry... I completely forgot to give you these keys... Sorry for making you wait for me.....Lu Jing : No-no.. Don't be sorry... It's alright..

In xin-ye's room......

Ximi : ummm... I have challenged that girl ( Suzi ) Xin-ye ( shocked ) : whatttt...... But why.... Ahhhhh....... Can't you just stay away from her... She isn't a good person.. ( worried )..Ximi : Yaaa I just couldn't handle her attitude.. the way she was talking like she is the only one who can play basketball. Xin-ye ( angry ) : So, you just challanged her.... Urghhhhh what do I do now huh?  You don't even know how to play basketball...Ximi ( gulped ) : ( in low voice ) but you know how to play... And we can't lose to her.. righ? Xin-ye ( deadly stare ) : How much time do we have ? Ximi : 2 days. Xin-ye : whattt? Before that Suzi I will kill you...Urghhhhh...... how am I supposed to teach you basketball in 2 days huh? ( takes deep breath ) ok never mind... If we start from today we have 3 days......Ximi : we have only 2 days including today ( scared smile )...Xin-ye ( angry ) : Ahhhhhh. Are you stupid or what huh?

On other side..Lu Jing was about to throw that cake box but he didn't throw it.

In Lu Jing's room...Lu Jing was staring that box...And a min later he smells the cake. Lu Jing ( vomit kinda expression ) : why Am I even smelling it... I should have throw it..

Lu Jing again started staring that box and after getting irritated by staring it.. He instantly picked the box and took a bite..Later he throws it.... ( coughing )...Why the hell did I even bother to taste this poison.

2 Days later.

At Ximi's classroom...Ximi : I am so scared what if I lost the match.... Ahhhhh....Xin-ye : I know you aren't prepared for it but you have to do it you have to show her that you can do it. And if you lose the match and somebody tried to make fun of you then you can tell me I will beat him. ( giggles )...Harry : Hey! What's up guys..Long time no see Xin-ye...Xin-ye : Yaaa someone is quite busy in bunking the classes..Harry : Umm it's just I don't like studies....( takes out one notebook from his bag ).. That's why I just copy the homework with my.... Charm...Xin-ye : charm...or ( smiles )Ximi : Oh wait. Isn't It my notebook... You thief.. How dare you steal my notebook huh? Ximi started running behind Harry..Xin-ye ( laughing ) : Yaaa guys stop it..... ( laughing ).

Ximi : ( got hurt by a desk ) ouch!.. Harry and Xin-ye immediately run towards Ximi. Ximi's leg started bleeding. Harry ( quite worried ) : Yaaa can't you even walk properly huh!? It looks quite deep...X in-ye : Yaaaa can't you be a bit careful while doing all this childish things huh !? ( Mimicking of Harry )Ximi : It's all his fault why did he steal my notebook and was running like a thief.

Harry ( worried ) : Let's go to the medical room...Ximi : Aishhh.. It's not a big deal... I just need a band-aid and it might be inside my bag pack let me check.... Ximi tried to walk but she fall back to the seat...Xin-ye ( worried ) : whatt happened?

Ximi ( nervous ) : I am not able to stand. It's like I can't even feel my leg... Harry/xin-ye : what? Yaaa don't prank on us like this ok..Ximi : I am not joking. Harry slaps on her leg.... Xin-ye also does some beating on her leg. But Ximi doesn't feel any pain or anything.

Harry : Let's go to the Medical...Xin-ye : but how she can't walk..Harry carried Ximi on his shoulders...Ximi : yaaa what are you doing.( Harry without listening to her started walking )Xin-ye also started going behind them.

Medical room

Nurse : I don't know what has happened to her cause it's a minor cut and she is saying she can't feel anything/pain. It's quite surprising so, we have to wait for the doctor..Xin-ye : oh ok.....

Ximi : oh no... I completely forgot... Ahhhhh Harry ( annoyed ) : What do you want now? Ximi : xin-ye that Suzi might think I am pretending... Ahhhhhhh why did this have to be happened today ( deadly stare to Harry ). ( grabs his collar ). Why did you steal my notebook huh? Xin-ye ( in mind : What's going on... And when did they become this close -smiles ).

Xin-ye: yaa stop it. And leave him it wasn't completely his fault... And as for Suzi I will talk to her. Ximi : But still she is such a bitc* she will surely do something to make me embarrassed...Xin-ye ( Smirked ) : Not today..Just leave everything on me...Xin-ye to Harry : Take care of her... I have to go now...Harry ( nodded ).

Xin-ye head back to her classroom.. Suzi intentionally tries to talk with Lu Jing but lu Jing didn't even gave a little bit of his attention to her.

Xin-ye saw all this ( from the entrence of the classroom ) and started smirking..Suzi saw Xin-ye smiling and got angry.

Suzi to Xin-ye : Stop smiling.. And I have heard that your so called bestie have got hurt... Don't you think she is pretending because she is scared of losing the match from me huh? Xin-ye : don't worry.. If she can't play with you I will play.. You can beat me in the match if you can...( smile ) >>left<<

Lu Jing ( looks at her suspiciously ) Suzi ( in anger went back to her seat ) : It's a good thing that you will be my competitor in today's match I will show you what I really am.

[ Yi han heard all this but doesn't show that he has heard anything or just behaves like he doesn't exist...But somehow Xin-ye always notices him and doesn't make him feel like he doesn't exist ]

After the Lunch bell.. Most of the students left to have their food..Yi han nervously goes to towards Xin-ye's desk....Xin-ye ( politely ) : umm... Do you want anything...Lu Jing was also there but not at his desk... He was just leaving but stopped after seeing them.

Yi han ( stummered ) : Su-suzi.. she isn't a g-good p-person.. I heard her saying that... She will s-show what she really is.. I kn-know that you guys are going to have a match... But I would like to say.... That you s-shouldnt play with h-her.

Xin-ye : Thanks for your concern. But I am sorry to say but I will play with her ( smiles ).

Lu Jing ( in mind : she is polite with everyone except me. She can smile and talk with everyone but with me...the only thing she can do is fighting... Urghhhhh when will she understands that she should maintain some distance with strangers ).

Xin-ye to Lu Jing : why are you still here? Aren't you going to have your lunch huh? Lu Jing : Why can't you be a bit more sensible huh?  Don't you understand that talking with a stranger whom we don't even know can be dangerous.

Xin-ye ( smirked ) : stranger...Aren't you also a stranger for me. Who is just using me... ( hurtful words )... I should be more careful when I am with you as you are a devil.. >>left<<

# CHAPTER 28

Xin-ye ( smirked ) : stranger.. Aren't you also a stranger for me.. Who is just using me... ( hurtful words ). I should be more careful when I am with you as you are a devil.... >>left<<

Xin-ye ( on her way ) : What did I say and why? urghhhhhh... it might have hurt him.. ( tapping her feet on the ground ).

Suzi : smirking.. yaaaa xin-ye, are you regretting...Xin-ye ( annoyed ) : regretting what? Suzi : Don't tell me you forgot about the challenge... be ready in the sports period. >>Left with a sarcastic smile<<

Xin-ye : Is she up to something? ( after a few steps ) Of course she is how can I forget.. urghhh.. she wants this necklace and for this she can do anything I should talk about this with Lu Jing. She turned back and started going towards the class. Suddenly stopped.. ahhhhhh.. I can't talk to him right especially after what I have said to him..What do I do now? Xin-ye started walking and thinking of a way to protect herself and the necklace.. Xin-ye ( happily ) : Harry he can help me.

In the medical room Harry : You are such a trouble maker...Ximi ( annoyed ) : I haven't asked you to stay here with me..you can go wherever you want to.

Xin-ye ( deep breath ) : They are still fighting... yaaaa you two stop it..and Harry, you come with me..Ximi : You are here for him..Very good... here an innocent person has got hurt but nobody cares...Xin-ye : Ohhh... someone is hurt...but still getting what she wants.. her favourite fruit ( points at the fruit basket) her favourite novel...huh? Ximi : Yaaa.. Xin-ye : huhh? ( smiles ) we will be back soon.

Xin-ye and Harry walking in the corridor...Xin-ye : I think Suzi have made a trap for me ( she explains him everything ). Harry : If it's the case then don't worry I will try my best to protect you from that bitch..Xin-ye : But be careful because she is not as straight as she looks.. ( She was walking while saying all this).

Harry jumped in front of Xin-ye to surprise her : meowwwww ...Xin-ye ( hand on her heart/chest ) : yaaa..... wanted to give me a heart attack huh? Harry : hehehe... Don't take tension dude you can do it... GOOD LUCK! Xin-ye : Thanks.

In the Sports period.

Everyone was gathered in the playground. The match was about to start..Someone : I will announce the rules...the one who will shoot 3 balls first will be the winner.

Suzi : streching her body.. You gonna regret it ( smirked ).

The match starts..Xin-ye and Suzi started playing.. the match was going smoothly.. Xin-ye scores the first goal..Suzi ( no expression ) : Impressive...Match continues... And now the score are 2:2.

Suzi : Last goal and your game over..Xin-ye : Let's see who's game is going to be over.

On the other hand Lu Jing was in the classroom as he didn't have any idea of this challenge between Xin-ye and Suzi... he just didn't want to be in the crowd so, he didn't go to the ground but heard he some noise and saw Xin-ye & Suzi playing from the window of the classroom.

Xin-ye jumped to throw the ball ( her necklace was hanging in air as she jumped ) and at this moment Suzi ( smirked that's what I wanted.) she grabbed Xin-ye's necklace.. as soon as Xin-ye reaches the ground, her necklace was gone.

Xin-ye won the match but lost her necklace..Xin-ye : ( grinding teeth ) You. Everyone started gathering around Xin-ye.. & Suzi took the advantage of it and left from there with a satisfied smile Harry went behind Suzi.

Lu Jing saw all this from the window he uses his powers to come to the ground.. Lu Jing ( loud voice ) : Principal is coming.. Everyone started panicking and went back to there classroom very quickly.

Xin-ye & Lin were still there.

Xin-ye standing stunned. Lin ( worried ) : Are you okay? ( shakes Xin-ye ). Xin-ye : huh? hn... I'm alright ( confused ) but according to the letter I should have died then why am I still alive ? Something is not right.

Lu Jing : You are alive cause she hasn't defeated you yet and that's why she can't even use the powers but you might have to pay the price.

Lin : when did you come here?

Lu Jing to Xin-ye ( a bit rudely ): If you had told me about all these things then the situation could have been something else.

Xin-ye ( avoiding eye contact ) : I know it's my fault and I'm really sorry sorry cause I can't help you anymore as I am not the necklace guardian anymore ( fake smile ) >> LEFT <<

Lu Jing was about to go behind Xin-ye but Lin stopped him..Lin : Don't go or she might feel more guilty let her be alone for a moment.

Lu Jing : She is already blaming herself.. if we don't do anything right now then her life will be in danger.

Lin : What do you mean? will she die? Lu Jing ( unhappy ) : Maybe.

Lin trying not to express his emotions.

Lu Jing ( in mind : both are same.......) : I have to go.

Lu Jing started searching for Xin-ye.. after searching for a few places he heard someone sobbing.

Lu Jing ( laugh ) : What are you doing here under staircase....are you trying to scare someone.

Xin-ye ( sobbing ) : I am useless ( childish face but cute  ). I was only able to help you but now, I can't even do that...Lu Jing ( calmly ) : You are useless... but not completely.

Xin-ye ( takes a deep breath ) : You know what you don't even know how to comfort someone and secondly you shouldn't waste your time on me I will be alright after few minutes.

Lu Jing ( a bit rudely ) : You think I don't know how to comfort someone...ohkk then swap our roles and teach me how to comfort someone.

Xin-ye : huh? Okay. I am going upstairs when I will pass from there you have to cry...ok? Lu Jing nodded.

Xin-ye started coming down from the stairs..Lu Jing ( started crying in loud voice like a small kid ). Xin-ye ( laugh ) : Stop it.... stop it... you have to cry according to your age if you will be this loud then the security guard will think someone have left their 3 years old child.

Lu Jing : ok ok.. let's do it again.

Xin-ye again came down... Her acting was quite good.. Xin-ye ( sadly ) : Hey why are you crying? Lu Jing ( real tears ) : I lost something...Xin-ye ( teary eyes ) : Are you crying for real.. she hugs him.

Lu Jing ( after a few seconds ) : Wait.. are you taking advantage of me huh? Xin-ye didn't move not even for a second.. Lu Jing : yaaa...( he noticed that Xin-ye's body has started heating up ) what's going on.. ( he is way too scared )...he uses his powers and teleport from school to his room.

He laid her down on the bed.

Lu Jing ( his hands were shaking ) : I know it's all my fault from the very beginning it's all my fault....but what can I do now.... I don't want her to die as she is innocent she didn't do anything wrong with anyone..( tears drop from his eye ) her condition and everything is my fault.. if I haven't had a crush on Suzi and if I hadn't plucked that flower everything would have great she would have been living her life peacefully.

Xin-ye opens her eyes... : Where I am? Lu Jing wipes his tears and turns back.

Lu Jing : it's my room. Xin-ye : But what are we doing here and my head is aching Lu Jing gets a call from Lin.

On call..Lin : Where are you and where is Xin-ye? Lu Jing : we are at my house don't worry she is safe here. Lin : I am coming. there is something very important which you have to know.. Lu Jing : What's that? >>Hangs up<<

Xin-ye: ahhhh.. my head it's like it will blast at anytime... ( grabbing her head way too tightly ) Lu Jing : It might be the side effects or..

Xin-ye : Or I might be going closer to my death right ? Lu Jing nodded : let me try my powers on you maybe it will reduce some of your pains he sits beside her and holds her head with both of his hands.

Xin-ye : Why don't you just do me a massage? Lu Jing : Massage won't help you cause it's not a normal headache you might have to bear more painful things and will die at the end if you don't get the necklace on time.

Xin-ye : Or Suzi will kill me cause she can only become the gaurdian after killing me ( smile ) Lu Jing ( holding his anger ) : You should have told me about all these things ( still holding her head and was healing her )Xin-ye : If I had told you earlier you won't let me do this challenge with her.

Lu Jing ( in mind : Of course I won't).

Xin-ye : by the way your powers are quite effective they have reduced almost all of my headache.

Door bell rings.

Lu Jing went to open the door.

Lin and Harry ( heavily breathing ) : Where is Xin-ye..Lu Jing : In my room.

In room.

Harry ( kind of scared ) : I followed Suzi.. I found that..Lin : He found an another Devil.

Xin-ye ( looks at Lu Jing surprisingly ) : 2 Devils. but how and who?

Harry : I couldn't see his face but he is an old and quite powerful devil even Suzi was scared of him she wasn't as brave as she shows herself in front of everyone she is just obeying all his orders.

Xin-ye : Why is everything getting this much complicate and who is this another Devil.

Harry : I don't know why but I am kinda way too scared even my ears are coming out frequently on my head and sometimes even my tail I can't go anywhere like this. Lin : I am even more scared ( stands beside xin-ye ) but I will save you.

Xin-ye ( laughs ) : You will save me huh? look a lizard. Lin ( scared ) : what? ( jumped on the bed ) where?! Xin-ye ( laughs ) : You were going to save me. Lin : Very funny.

Lu Jing : Harry was there something you noticed and found weird.

Harry ( thinks for a while ) : um... yeah one thing which I found suspicious was.. I saw.

Writer : I know this story is kinda being boring but I will try to make it interesting as before.

# CHAPTER 29

Lu Jing : Harry, was there something you noticed or found weird.

Harry ( thinks for a while ) : um.. yeah one thing which I found suspicious was. I saw blood. I didn't see his face but I saw blood in his hand ( raised his voice ). And a watch an old watch. From this we can find out who was that devil.

Lu Jing : It won't be enough ( kind of scared and tensed ). Right now we have to find that necklace.. so that she can stay alive.

Lin : We can ask Suzi about that necklace.. I mean lu Jing we scare her by using his devilish powers and Harry can also use his powers.

Harry : I think we have to do this, as we don't have any other option nor enough time to come up with a whole new plan.

Later.

At Suzi's house..Suzi's mom : Suzi isn't at home. You guys can wait for her if it's urgent to meet her... She might be on her way back home .

They were waiting for Suzi and suddenly Suzi's mom's phone rang.

Suzi's mom ( on call ) : what?  ( shocked ) no, this not possible ( falls on the floor and started crying ) Everyone gets worried and ask Suzi's mom : What happened Aunt? Is everything ok?

Suzi's mom ( crying ) : They are saying that my daughter has died.

Everyone ( shocked ) : whatt?!  But how Harry : I mean.. There might be some confusion.

Suzi's mom ( sobbing ) : yeah! You are right, my daughter can't die.

Door bell rings ...Xin-ye and others get worried.

Cops ( low voice ) : We have found a dead body. Please check if she is your daughter.. or not.

Everyone saw Suzi's dead body [ dead body : it was like some animals have tried to eat her alive. There were many scratches on her body..the body's condition was not likely to be seen]

Lu Jing covers Xin-ye's eyes but xin-ye had already seen her dead body.

Suzi's mom was crying badly..Harry and Lin were trying to console her.

Xin-ye ( her eyes filled with tears ) : what happened with her? ( hides herself in lu Jing's arms ). Please take me somewhere else ( Trying to control herself from crying ). Lu Jing ( covers her in his arms and after looking around he disappeared from there ).

Night scene..They came to a hill...Xin-ye started vomiting.. Lu Jing patting on her back .. And notices that she is vomiting blood.

Lu Jing ( panicked ) : Are you ok? Ahhh.. The things are getting more complicated...Xin-ye : Don't blame yourself, you did nothing wrong... and about Suzi ( got a sudden flashback and got scared ). I don't want to die like her ( teary eyes ).

Lu Jing suddenly hides xin-ye behind himself and attacks someone in the sky.. Xin-ye ( coughing ) : whom are you attacking?

Lu Jing ( holding his hand in air - using his powers ) : Stay behind me and hold me tightly. Don't you dare to leave me.

( laughing ) : you think you can hide her... Nahh you can't.. And you ( very politely ) wanna come with me? I will give you whatever you want.. And also this necklace ( necklace visible in sky ).

Xin-ye : Did you kill Suzi? : Yes, cause she stole this necklace from you.. She tried to put your life in danger.. Which is not acceptable not at all... I will kill everyone who will try to harm you.

Lu Jing : And I will kill you.. Xin-ye : let me handle him.. She tried to come in front but lu Jing grabbed her hand and hides her behind him.. Lu Jing : Don't go ahead.. Stay here.

Xin-ye : okay I won't go anywhere... And you Mr old devil.. If you don't want to harm me then why are you attacking on us ? And I don't want anyone to die just because of me... Can't you just let Suzi stay alive.

: You want that Suzi to come back to life? Xin-ye nodded with nervous face. : As you wish... She will be alright you can meet her tonight but not tomorrow cause I will send her somewhere else and I will erase all her memories about you and necklace.

Xin-ye ( shocked ) : You can make her alive ? ( looks at Lu Jing ).

:yeah! I can do anything.. And here's your necklace please wear it and stay alive.. Cause I can't give lives to guardians, angels and demons ( rudely ) : And you Little devil.. Stay away from her.

Lu Jing : You better stay away from us ( tightening his grab on Xin-ye's hand ). Or I will kill you.

( laughs ) : oh really? Let's see who will kill whom ( politely ) have a good rest princess. We will meet soon.

Lu Jing/ Xin-ye : princess.

Suddenly xin-ye started something in her neck it was her necklace.

Xin-ye : Don't tell me he is in love with me or something like that..Lu Jing ( angry ) : Stop thinking these nonsenses.. And don't you ever dare to talk to him, if he ever appears like this again you must call me.

Xin-ye ( weird look ) : okay ( suddenly ) oh yeah. Let's go to Suzi's house.. Faster.. Use your powers and go there.

At Suzi's house.

Xin-ye : why is there so much crowd here?

Lin : finally I saw you. You know what everyone was trying to console Suzi's mom and suddenly Suzi wake up and started searching for food I literally got scared.. I think she is not Suzi but a ghost.

Xin-ye ( takes a deep breath ) : Good to hear that. Now I can finally sleep peacefully...Lin : huh?

Lu Jing ask Lin to come with him..Lu Jing : You know I am a devil and I can even kill you right! So, I want you to stay with your sister 24/7 don't leave her alone not even for a second with anyone... And bring me that diary ( the diary which she got from the priest - in which everything has written what has happened till now ).

Lin ( gulped ) : Why do I feel like you are trying to scare me..Lu Jing : You already know that there is an another Devil who is trying to get closer to Xin-ye.

Lin : what? What does he want from her? Lu Jing : Do what I have asked you to.. And i will take care of the rest.. Call me if anything happens okay...Lin ( nodded ).

Few weeks later.

In school.

Class Teacher : Students as you know that the annual function is going to be celebrated in 2 next week.. So, I hope you guys have participated in some activities I want you all to participate in some activities as it's your school era which won't come back again.. you guys must have some good memories of your school life so, make some memorable days.. But don't forget that you can't let your studies get affected by all these things.. ALL THE BEST.

Lin : we haven't participated in anything yet.. Xin-ye : Let's decide something In lunch time... ( looks at Lu Jing ) will you join us?

Yi-han ( comes to Xin-ye s desk ) : Can I join you? ( innocently )Xin-ye : Sure ( smiles ).

Lu Jing & Lin were staring her and got angry with her...Xin-ye: Why are you making faces like this?  He wanted to join us so, I just let him joined us..Lu Jing was staring her quite weirdly.

Xin-ye ( blinking her eyes ) : yaaa stop staring at me like this.. It's like you will eat me from your eyes.

Lu Jing : If you want me to join you then you have to remove him..Xin-ye : then don't join us simple.

Lu Jing : what the hell? You just asked me to join you and now you are... Urghhh you are such a..

Xin-ye: such a what? Huh?? ( started getting angry and getting closer to Lu Jing )...Why are you not completing your sentence.. Huh?

[ everyone in the classroom started staring at them ]Lu Jing : I will join you and you have to kick that ( side eye on Yi-han ) Guy.

Xin-ye : If you want to join me then you have to co-operate with him.. Or else you can choose not to join me I don't care...Lin : yaaa what are you doing? Everyone is looking at both of you..Xin-ye : huh?? ( she realised that she is very close to Lu Jing ). Her heartbeat started getting faster.. Her cheeks turned red.. Started feeling the heat in her body.

Lu Jing Smirked.

At lunch break.

Xin-ye, lu jing, Lin , Harry , Ximi and Yi-han were gathered at a table.

Some other students also were there who were interested in joining them.

Lu Jing didn't want Yi-han to be in their team so, he tried to use his powers but didn't succeed..Xin-ye and Ximi were distributing roles for their drama.

Everything was going smoothly...After school they decided to meet at Harry's apartment for rehearsal.

They started practicing their role...Ximi : Bro.. Your deskmate is just perfect.. Look at him he have recited all the lines and his expressions and everything - no words...Xin-ye ( in mind : He is perfect.. But Not me ). : let's practice our roles.

On Annual Day.

Dressing room..Xin-ye and others were getting ready. Everyone was looking quite good...Ximi : Bro you are looking so natural and pretty especially your eyes ( doe eyes ). Why am I looking like a dumb..ugh. Xin-ye ( nervous ) : just tell me nah.... That you want me to appreciate you... You are looking perfect now let's go out.

Xin-Ye & Ximi went out to meet others.

Other boys : Woah…She is looking so pretty dude…Lu Jing didn't know that they were talking about xin-ye he was busy in his phone he didn't even glance at Xin-ye while xin-ye was waiting for his one glance.

Lin : woahh.. You are looking like a witch today ( laugh )..Xin-ye : Hahah very funny.

Lu Jing saw Xin-ye and his eyes got stuck on her.. But xin-ye didn't notice…Yi-han ( soft voice ) : You are so pretty…Lu Jing ( started getting angry ) : ( in mind : Why is he interfering in her business..he is really irritating me ).

The performance starts..They gave a great performance on the stage… Later when Xin-ye came back in the dressing room she found a letter. She thought it might be from other students. But it was from another Devil.

Letter : You are looking very pretty today. I saw your performance and it was fabulous. We will meet soon. Don't forget me my princess.

Xin-ye ( nervous )…Lu Jing ( knocks on the door )..: If you haven't changed yet, then come out for a photo shoot…Xin-ye : You come inside.. Faster..Lu Jing : huh? He came inside..Xin-ye showed him that letter.

# CHAPTER 30

Xin-ye : You come inside.. Faster...Lu Jing : huh? He came inside..Xin-ye showed him that letter..Lu Jing ( in mind : He is Literally irritating me.. >>Controls his anger<< ).Xin-ye : I think he is still here..Lu Jing ( slowly slowly crushing that letter ). : Let's go out for the photos, we will find him later.

Xin-ye ( tired ) : ( sneezing )..ohk.. Let's go..Lu Jing : You have cold ? ( About to give her his jacket )..Xin-ye : Not yet... Let's finish this photo shoot and go home early.

Everyone was taking their photos and shooting some videos for memories.

A boy : you two should take a photo together as you two are looking like a couple...Lin ( started laughing ) : Them.. Couple?..( Laugh )..What a joke dude...They would rather kill each other.

Ximi : I don't think so... I think they can do anything for ea-chother.

Xin-ye ( sneezing ) : What the hell? ( sneeze ) are you guys talking ( Sneeze ).

Yi-han and Lu Jing both offered a tissue at the same time.

Everyone was waiting for Xin-ye to take Lu Jing's tissue as they were shipping them.

Xin-ye ( cough ) and takes another tissue from the table.

Everyone made faces...A girl : I wish lu Jing had offered that tissue to me .. I would have framed it.. A boy : What's so special about him... Huh? I don't know why but you girls are crazy about him ( Annoyed ).

Few weeks later.

[ They got 1 Month holiday]

At Xin-ye's house.. Xin-ye was having her breakfast and got a message from Lu Jing...Message : Let's find that another Devil during these holidays.....Xin-ye text back : Ok ( excited ).. Xin-ye ( in mind : Finally there will be some fun ).

Later.

Xin-ye was waiting for lu Jing outside his house... And met Yi-han..Yi-han ( nervous ) : hey.. What are doing here? Xin-ye : Hey .. Um I live here.. What about you? Yi-han : I-I came to meet my uncle... He lives here.

Lu Jing came and saw them and got angry : what the hell he is doing here I don't know why but he and that Devil is annoying me a lot.

Lu Jing ( with long steps goes towards xin-ye ) : Let's go we are getting late... ( Grabbed her hands and started going.

Xin-ye : yaa...... Bye Yi-han ( smiled )...Yi-han ( surprised ) : huh! Oh bye.

Xin-ye : What was that huh? Don't you have manners? Lu Jing ( still holding her hand ) : I don't.. Any problem.. ( Stopped walking ).

Xin-ye ( friendly tone ) : your behaviour today is quite different...( Touched his forehead to check his temperature ). Lu Jing ( removed her hand from his forehead ) their eyes meet.. Lu Jing : Let's get rid of that Devil first..Xin-ye: hmm... Ok.. But from where will we start our research huh?

Lu Jing : I don't know.. Xin-ye ( surprised ) : what? Then where are we going? Lu Jing : use your powers to see invisible black footsteps... If we find any black footprints then we will follow them.. Xin-ye : huh? Invisible black footprints... Wait let me try to see it.. ( Uses her powers and shouted with happiness ) . I found it.... Woahhh.... Look here.

Lu Jing : Stupid... That's my footprints...Xin-ye ( disappointed ) : huhhh? that means your's and that devil's footprint have same coloured footsteps... Then how will we find him? What if we couldn't identify those footprints?

Lu Jing : That's why it's quite challenging. And didn't you say you want to have fun. Now, have fun while finding those footprints... Xin-ye ( deep breath ) : Let's start our work.

It's been an Hour since they started searching for footprints.

Lu Jing : I don't think we would find him like this... Xin-ye : I am just getting frustrated.... ( Suddenly ) yaaaa... How can we forget that we have Harry... He can find those footprints easily... Let me call him.

Xin-ye called Harry...Xin-ye : hey.... Harry I need your help can you come here? Ximi ( surprised ) : Xin-ye is that you? Xin-ye : Ximi? Ximi : hmm....Xin-ye : what? Wait where is Harry and what are you doing with him huh? Xin-ye and Lu Jing got suspicious.

[ Flash back of Ximi & Harry ]

[ Harry and Ximi saw eachother on the road... The time when Ximi recognised Harry.. Harry tried to run but Ximi called him and ran behind him.

After running for a while Ximi grabbed his collar from behind.

Harry : urghh... Why it's her again? ( Turned ) Ximi ( shocked ) : staring at Harry's head... These fake ears are so cute... ( Makes fun of him ). So, you ran because you didn't want me to see you in these cute cat ears hairband huh? Harry ( surprised ) : ( in mind : what is she saying?)

Ximi touched his ears and tried to take it off...Harry : ouchh.. Urghhh how can you pull someone's ears like this.. ( Grabbed her ears). Ximi ( angry ) : yaa.... Leave my ears... I am not pulling your real ears so, leave my ears.

Harry ( realise that his cat ears have came out.. And notices that his tail is also visible but Ximi haven't noticed it yet).

Ximi ( angry ) : youuuu. Aish leave it...( started going on her way).

Harry grabbed her collar from behind..: come with me I will give you food.

Ximi : huh? do you think I am pet ? Harry : ok boss now let's go home.. ( He was just using Ximi as a shield to protect himself from others ).

At Harry's house...Harry opened his house door... And before he could say something he turned into a cat.

Ximi ( shocked ) : screamed..Harry ( shocked ) : me-owwwwwwwww.

After few minutes..Harry ( in cat form tried to approach her but Ximi was so stunned to say anything..) : Meowwwww...

Ximi ( nervous ) : w-ho are you? ( Tries not to go closer to him) Harry : I am a demon... A cat demon..Ximi ( ultra shocked cause it was her first time seeing a person converted into a cat and the talking cat in real life.. It wasn't realistic at all..): gulped...You can even talk.

Harry : wait for few more minutes...I will explain you when I will become a human being.

After few minutes of silence Harry finally came back to his human form..

Ximi ( scared + not making eye contact )...: You are not a human being but I don't know whether you will harm me or not.

Harry : first of all you can't tell anyone about what has happened today..Secondly I am not a bad person.. It's just I am not like a normal human beings... You don't have to be scared of me.... ( Going closer to Ximi... Ximi got more scared ). You have to keep it a secret or else no one knows what I can do ( develish smirked ).

Harry turned on the tv and sits beside Ximi.

Ximi was thinking something.

After a while.

Ximi : umm...Can I ask you something? Harry nodded...( Drinking water). Ximi : Can you make me a cat demon like you? Please.

Harry ( threw all the water out and started coughing...) : ( still coughing.....) You want to be cat demon? What the hell...( Coughs..)Went to the washroom]

Ximi to Xin-ye : it's a long story... And what were you talking about huh? What help?

Xin-ye ( tries to cover up a lie ) : umm... I was...I wanted Harry to teach something in chemistry...( Takes a deep breath )Ximi : Bro.. Why the hell are you studying right now stupid...Just enjoy nah.. This is our last break just enjoy it.

Xin-ye: umm.. you are right I won't waste my vacation ( fake smile ) ( Hangs up )..Urghh.

Lu Jing : We don't need him.. My powers are enough to find that Devil but I am not sure whether I should take you there or not... Xin-ye held Lu Jing's hand and dragged him and hid themselves behind a gaint rock.

Xin-ye ( covered his mouth) : just be quite.. It's my dad's car. And I can't let him see me like this. cause he is with one of his colleagues.

Lu Jing was staring at her face.

Xin-ye : Finally they have gone...Lu Jing saw the car... And got surprised : this car... It has been touched by that devil..Xin-ye: huh? what do you mean?

Lu Jing : We have to follow that car...Xin-ye : don't need to follow them.. They are going to my house...And if that colleague is devil then we will kill him ok ?

Lu Jing ( surprised ) : ( in mind : Does she think that killing a devil is so simple... Ughhh... Why am I stuck with this stupid ).

On the other hand

Ximi : hey! ( Politely ) Can I become a cat? ( Petty eyes )Harry : ofcourse not I was born like this.. And why do you even want to be a cat ?

Ximi : cause I love cats... And ( remember something). Wait.. When you were in cat form you were just same as Xin-ye's cat. ..Does Xin-ye know about you huh?

Harry : ( in mind : She isn't that stupid.. But still I can't tell her everything).

# CHAPTER 31

At Xin-ye's house.

Xin-ye's Dad and his colleague were talking in the hall.. Xin-ye comes inside the hall with Lu Jing...Xin-ye ( excitedly & emotionally ) : Dad.. ( Notices uncle )... Greets Uncle..Lu Jing also greets them..Colleague/Uncle : Hi xin-ye... It's been a long time... How are you? Xin-ye ( suspiciously ) : I am all good..I think I should not disturb you.. Dad I have a lot of things to discuss with you. I missed you so much ( emotionally ). Dad : I missed you too my princess.

Lin ( came from outside ) : What about me? you only missed your witch huh? Xin-ye kicked Lin and then realised that there is a guest.. She behaved herself.

Dad, lu Jing and uncle started laughing.

They had some more conversation..Xin-ye introduced Lu Jing as her good friend and many more things.

In Xin-ye's room.

Xin-ye : I don't think he is devil..Lu Jing : Neither me... But there's that mark ( looks at the car from the window ) is still there..Xin-ye : But there are no black footprints...Lu Jing : That's why it's suspicious.

Lin ( confused and his expressions were quite funny ) : What footprints? What's suspicious huh?.. Are you guys even going to explain me anything or not huh? --------ignored-------

Xin-ye : So, what's our next plan? Lu Jing : I am not sure.

Lin : yaaaaa ( shouted )  at least tell me something. Maybe I can give you some ideas...Xin-ye : Yaaa shut your mouth.. Xin-ye explained him everything.... Now tell me your idea..Lin ( fake smile ) : No Idea.. Hehhee.

Lu Jing : yaaa You have that letter right? Xin-ye : which letter? Lu Jing : That one...who told us to find demons..Xin-ye: Yeah.. But I don't know where it is...Lin ( disappointed look in a childish way ) : Have you ever kept something carefully.

Xin-ye : hahaha very funny... ( Looks at the wall clock). Yaaa devil it's getting late you should go back to your house... I will look for that Letter and inform you ck..Lu Jing : ohk... Be careful.

In hall...Dad : Are you going back to your house? Lu Jing nodded with a polite smile...Dad : I heard that you are her ( points at Xin-ye's mom.. ) Bestfriend's son... And also tutoring Xin-ye.

Lu Jing ( kind of getting nervous ) : ummm... That's true... I have been tutoring her since last semester..Dad  : That's impressive...It's a quite hard job to teach her.. Thanks.. Lu Jing ( don't know what to say ).. Nodded.

Dad : One more thing.. Tomorrow is Xin-ye and Lin's birthday... You are invited.

Lu Jing got surprised and looked at Xin-ye, who was herself surprised.

Lin : I nearly forgot that tomorrow is my birthday..Xin-ye : me too...Oh I got it, that's why you came today otherwise you would be back after 2 days right?

Dad ( smiled ).. Mom : Now you should go... Your mom must be waiting for you Lu Jing nodded and left.

At Midnight.

Xin-ye and Lin celebrated their birthday with their parents.

After that little celebration they both get back to their room s...Xin-ye was quite happy but when she reached in her room... She saw a big flower bouquet with a card..and also that black footprints...She immediately called Lu Jing without thinking twice.

Xin-ye : Come to my room.. Those black footprints I can see them..Lu Jing : huh... If he have left something then stay away from that... Ok and don't be scared..Xin-ye ( excited ) : I am not scared...I am just too excited.... Come faster.... >> Hangs up <<Lu Jing ( weird expression ) : She isn't a human... Urghh...

In Xin-ye's room...Xin-ye was waiting for Lu Jing excitedly.... Xin-ye : I wish today's day to be the most adventurous day.

As soon as Xin-ye said these lines.. Her room started changing it's shape... Xin-ye got scared + excited...Her surroundings turned into a forest.

On the other hand when Lu Jing came to her room ( her normal room )... He didn't find Xin-ye anywhere...Lu Jing : Was she pranking on me or something... He notices that black footprints.... He thought of following it but before he could do something he saw the letter on follower bouquet....Letter : Hi birthday girl.. This flower isn't a normal flower, you can ask whatever you want and it will make your wish come true.. Enjoy your day.

Lu Jing : This stupid girl... Urghhh she must have said something nonsense... Why the hell I am stuck with her.. ( Frustrated ).

Lu Jing ( thinks for a moment ) : Take me to Xin-ye.

Xin-ye : yaaa devil is this you... Lu Jing : Where are you? Xin-ye : I don't know.. My room just turned into a forest maybe aur I am just somewhere.. ( confused )...Lu Jing : Make a wish saying that I want Lu Jing join me.. Xin-ye : but why.. Umm whatever... I want Lu Jing join me..

Her room again started turning..

Xin-ye : waohh.... You are here ( excitedly )Lu Jing ( angry ) : haven't I asked to stay away from his things..

Xin-ye : I didn't touch anything... I haven't even checked that bouquet..Lu Jing : Then did you made a wild wish..Xin-ye : umm.. Wild wish? Wait is this my wish? ( Got more excited ) woahh... That means it's going to be more adventurous.

Lu Jing : Urghh...I really can't stay with you.. You are just. Xin-ye ( angry ) : Sorry for disturbing your sleep... Sorry for calling you at this late hours... You can go.

Xin-ye : I wish Lu Jing to go back to his house and have a good sleep.

After few seconds....Xin-ye : why are you still here? Just now when I made a wish it was accomplished in just few seconds..Lu Jing : Cause this time you made your wish in anger.. And this flower only accept those wishes which are asked happily...

Xin-ye didn't reply..

Suddenly everything started shaking and the bats started flying here and there.

Xin-ye & Lu Jing started running...Lu Jing tried to hold her hand but Xin-ye didn't let him hold them.

Lu Jing forcefully grabbed her hands and started running even faster.

The surroundings again started changing.

Xin-ye & Lu Jing stopped and realised that it's their school.

On Blackboard : Happy Birthday Xin-ye.. But here's a bad news for you I have changed your adventurous wish into a horrible death wish.... Hope you enjoy your last birthday... You have 3 hours.. If you can go out from here then you can survive or else you will die.

Lu Jing : Was this also your wish? Xin-ye : No.. but that Devil he didn't want to kill me right? Even last time he gave me my necklace back.. Lu Jing : You really believe him that he isn't bad.

Xin-ye ( ignoring tone ) : You are also a Devil but you are not a bad person...Lu Jing didn't say anything...They both started finding a way to get out from here.

As soon as they move further they heard some weird voices... They both followed that voice and meet a monster looking so disgusting...The monster started attacking on them.. And they both started defending themselves..The no. Of monsters starting increasing and they got stuck with them.

While fighting...Xin-ye : It would be great if they were demons rather than Monster... Then I would have collected more demons.

Lu Jing : It has already been 2 hours.... By the way Do you have any death wish? Xin-ye : It won't be any harm even if I die.... But If I have to choose between you and me to die... Then I will choose you..Cause I don't like you not at all.

Lu Jing : Hahaha... Here I am trying to save you and you are finding a way to kill me so ungrateful...Xin-ye : hehhe...Concentrate on these monster so, that we can leave from here as soon as possible.

Lu Jing : They are so many and if they will attack like this then it's impossible for us to leave this place.

Xin-ye ( looks around ) : yaa can you fly? Lu Jing : Your imagination is so wild.. Wait I can fly... But why? Xin-ye : we can jump from this building and will easily got out from here...Lu Jing : I don't think it will be this much easy yeah but we can try..In count of 3.. hold me tightly ok.

Lu Jing & Xin-ye ( fighting with monsters ) : 1...2..and ..3.

They both jumped.... Firstly they fell then started flying in the sky.

Xin-ye : look.. We are safe now.. ( Smiled )..Lu Jing smile : Yeahh for the first time.. ( Noticed something ) or maybe not...

The fire balls started falling from the sky.

Lu Jing started losing his balance.. : Don't leave me or else you will fall...Xin-ye : Firstly protect yourself.

Lu Jing even got hurt because of those balls... Xin-ye started feeling guilty..Xin-ye : These Fire balls are trying to attack me not you.. So, it's better to fall from here.. ( She released herself from Lu Jing's grip and started falling).

Lu Jing with full speed grabbed Xin-ye's hand... ( Fast heartbeat ) : Are you out of your mind huh?

Xin-ye saw fire balls coming towards lu Jing before they could even touch him... Xin-ye uses all her strength to make a shield.

Xin-ye's eyes were closed as she was using all her strength just to save lu jing & herself.. She successfully made a shield. Xin-ye opened her eyes and got scared to see Lu Jing's face which was looking so horrible... It was like he will eat her raw.

Xin-ye's heartbeat got faster.. Lu Jing opens his mouth and his teeth came out like a vampire's teeth.. He moved closer to her neck and almost bit her.

# Epilogue

Xin-ye's heartbeat got faster... Lu Jing opens his mouth and his teeth came out like a vampire's teeth... He moved closer to her neck and almost bit her.

Xin-ye ( stummered + scared ) : what-what are you doing? Lu Jing ( smirked ) : ( heavy voice ) I will kill you.. ( and he sinks his teeth into her neck and starts sucking her blood).

Xin-ye ( in pain ) : Are you really Lu Jing?..Lu Jing ( stopped sucking her blood ) : I am the devil inside him who is thirsty.( Laughs ) and your blood is so tasty... I won't suck your all blood at once Yeahh.. But I will suck is slowly slowly.

Xin-ye fainted.

Few Hours later...Xin-ye wake up with a headache... She tried to process what happened last night.. And remembered everything.. ..She immediately ran towards the mirror and saw that mark on her neck....She suddenly started feeling weakness....Xin-ye wanted to Lu Jing but she was scared because of what happened last night.

Xin-ye continuously was thinking about Lu Jing. She heard someone's voice. ( Invisible ) : Happy Birthday Xin-ye...Xin-ye (

bravely ) : Who are you ? You are the one who sent me to that imaginary world right? : Yeah..... And I am really sorry about what happened last night.. I didn't expected that some other dark powers holder will try to kill you there or else I would have never given you that wish fulfilling bouquet... But I have already taught them a good lesson ( satisfied tone ). Xin-ye : What about Lu Jing? Where is he? : You have already seen everything what he did last night right? Then why are worried about him... You have no idea how dangerous he is right now for you.. I would advise you to stay away from him, he have already tasted your blood and he will get addicted to your blood if he again tastes your blood.

Xin-ye ( suspiciously ) : huh? What do you mean? And why does he want my blood? : Cause he neither have killed anyone or done anything wrong yet.. While devils are usually cold hearted and likes to torture others... That's why his inner dark side is becoming thirsty and wanted to kill you at that moment but Lu Jing tried his best to not kill you still sucked your blood... Your blood will keep him calm.. But he can kill anyone anytime.. ( Trying to scare her ).

Xin-ye : That means you also wants to kill me right or might want this necklace? : At first I wanted to kill you.. But Now... Xin-Ye : Thanks for the informations... And If you want to gift me something then stay away from me and my family... ( A sad smile ) : This wish can't be granted... See you later.

( Door knock ) Xin-ye stares the door and then opens it..Lin : Dad is asking you to come down.. ( Low voice ) Happy Birthday....Xin-ye lost in her thoughts and ignored what he said.

Lin ( shouted near her ears ) : Dad is calling..( Noticed her neck mark ) What's that? ( Got worried ). Xin-ye ( covers her neck ) : Nothing... Let's go dad is calling us right? Lin : But you have the ability to heal your wounds...Xin-ye ignores him and went downstairs.

Lin started having negative feelings.. And he calls Lu Jing.

Meanwhile..Lu Jing was looking at himself in a mirror... He was noticing the changes in his body.. And recalled what he did last night to Xin-ye.. ( Looks at his teeth in mirror ). His eyes started filling with tears.

Lu Jing ( started throwing his stuff ) : Why? Why is it happening to me? What wrong have I done ? Why ( cried ) I have always tried not to hurt anyone but still. I was about to kill her.. She have always helped me.

( His phone rings )...He looks at the caller ID: Lin.... ( His hand started shivering ) Lin : yaa Lu Jing.. Do you know what... I think something has happened with Xin-ye.... There is a weird mark on Xin-ye's neck which isn't healing... Lu Jing didn't replied....Lin : hey.. Are you there? After a while he hangs up the call.

Lu Jing Went downstairs. Lu Jing : Mom... ( He wanted to ask her mom if he can change the school or something like that so that he can stay away from Xin-ye ).

Mom ( was talking to someone ) : Ok.. So, let's do it next week...Mom : Son I have a bad news for you... We have to shift to another city because your Dad is coming back from abroad this week.. I am sorry I know you wanted to stay here but I can't do anything.. Lu Jing : We are snifting this week right?

Mom ( surprised ) : nodded..Are you ok with this?..Lu Jing ( slight smile ) : hmm.... I am going to pack my stuffs...Mom : Lu Jing.. Today is Xin-ye's birthday and you won't be able to meet her after a few  days... So, spend some quality time with your friends...Lu Jing stayed stunned.

At Night..Xin-ye's parents had organised a party for both of their children birthday.... Everyone was invited.... Lu Jing also go there but he was feeling quite guilty so, he doesn't go near Xin-ye.. Xin-ye knew that he is regretting what he did. But she knew that wasn't his intentions.

After cake cutting...Xin-ye asked Lu Jing to come with her..At first Lu Jing rejected to go with her... But she dragged her to the terrace... Xin-ye : You don't have to feel sorry... And i Know that it wasn't your intention....Meanwhile....Lu Jing's mind started getting out of his control... He started having many thoughts like kill her, no she isn't a bad person.. I am not a bad person.. I can't kill her.. ( His head was about to blast ). His eyes got stuck on her neck ( that mark ) Lu Jing ( smirked ).

Xin-ye ( notices his eyes ) . Lu Jing again came closer to her to suck her blood but this time... Xin-ye uses her powers to stops him...They had a fight...While xin-ye was protecting herself she was also saying some things which could affect Lu Jing to back to his senses.. Which really helped her.

Lu Jing ( frustrated ) : STAY AWAY FROM ME... >> Left <<His eyes again filled with tears.. He immediately got back to his house..And started packing his stuffs.

NEXT DAY..In early morning... Lu Jing's Mom : Where are you going? Lu Jing : Mom I am going to our new house.. I have talked with dad.. Mom : But.. ( Saw his son's pale face ). Lu Jing : Mom.. Dad will be back by tonight and you guys will also be there in 2-4 days...Mom : Ok. But please be careful ok... Lu Jing nodded.

On the other hand..This was the first time when Xin-ye woke up at early morning and was going to throw the garbage... ( Sleepyhead ) Talking to herself : Why did mom wake me up to throw all this garbage in this early morning.. She could have asked Lin. ( Yawning )... ( Saw Lu Jing.. ) Xin-ye and Lu Jing's eyes meet.

Xin-ye waved her hand with a sleepy face ( lu Jing ignored her ) she didn't notice his luggage or anything.. Xin-ye ( sleepy tone ) : He is so rude..

They both went back to their way.

Few Days later...Xin-ye got to know that Lu Jing and his family had moved to another City.

Xin-ye & Lin were quite shocked cause Lu Jing was staying here because he wanted to become a human being... Which only can be happened after finding 999 demons... But he left in middle of everything.

Xin-ye tried to contact Lu Jing but nothing happened.

Their school reopened... Everything is normal but still something is missing... Xin-ye has her powers but there is no one who would attack her to get the necklace.. Not even a demon or something unrealistic happened after that day.. Her life becomes the same as it was before.

The days passed like this....Xin-ye told everything to Ximi about the necklace, powers and etc... Ximi & Harry's bonding got even stronger and they started understanding each other but their teasing and fighting is still the same.

Xin-ye & Harry usually play with their powers and entertain Lin and Ximi. Everyone was happy but still Xin-ye was missing Lu Jing.

Entrance Exam Day....Xin-ye and others were quite nervous for their Entrance Exam as it's the most important exam of their life.. After Lu Jing left Xin-ye studied by her own.... She prepared for the exams.

Her school life ended.